GEORGE LAYTON

The Trick

and Other Stories

MACMILLAN CHILDREN'S BOOKS

'The Promise' first published
by Macmillan Children's Books in *War* 2004

This collection first published 2006 by Macmillan Children's Books
a division of Macmillan Publishers Limited
20 New Wharf Road, London N1 9RR
Basingstoke and Oxford
www.panmacmillan.com

Associated companies throughout the world

ISBN: 978-0-330-44161-2

5 7 9 8 6 4

A CIP catalogue record for this book is available from
the British Library.

Typeset by Intype Libra Ltd.
Printed and bound in Great Britain by
CPI Group Ltd (UK), Croydon CR0 4YY

For Gordon Roddick,
with affection

Acknowledgements

'Happy Birthday' words and music by Patty S. Hill and Mildred Hill copyright © 1935 (renewed 1962), Summy-Birchard Music, a division of Summy-Birchard Inc., USA. Reproduced by kind permission of Keith Prowse Music Publishing Co. Ltd, London WC2H 0QY

'On the Good Ship Lollipop' words and music by Sidney Clare and Richard A. Whiting copyright © 1934, Movietone Music Corp./EMI April Music Inc., USA. Reproduced by permission of Sam Fox Publishing Co. (London) Ltd/EMI Music Publishing Ltd, London WC2H 0QY

'We'll Meet Again' words and music by Ross Parker and Hughie Charles copyright © 1939 Dash Music Company Ltd. Used by permission of Music Sales Ltd. All Rights Reserved. International Copyright Secured

Children are blind to sarcasm – they take it as truth

– Overheard on a train

CONTENTS

THE PROMISE

'This is the BBC Light Programme.'

'Come on, Doreen, it's on!'

It's the same every Thursday night. We have to get our tea finished, clear the table, get the pots washed and put away so we can all sit round the wireless and enjoy *ITMA* with Tommy Handley.

'Doreen! She does it every time, goes out to the lavatory just as it's starting.'

Except I don't enjoy it. I can't understand it. I don't know what they're talking about.

'Tell her to hurry up, will you, love?'

I went out the back to call my Auntie Doreen but she was already coming up the path pulling on her black skirt. She'd come straight from work.

'He's not on yet, is he?'

He was. I could hear the audience on the wireless cheering and clapping the man who'd just shouted, '*It's That Man Again!*'

'Just startin', I think.'

She ran past me into the house.

'Freda, why didn't you call me?'

'I did.'

I can't understand what they get so excited about. They all come out with these stupid things like, '*I don't mind if I do,*' '*Can I do you now, sir?*' '*Tee tee eff enn.*' What's funny about that? Don't mean a thing to me.

'What's funny about that, Mum? "*Tee tee eff enn*"? It doesn't even mean owt.

'*Ta Ta For Now!*'

'*Ta Ta For Now!*'

They both sang it at me, laughing like anything.

'It's a catchphrase. Now shush!'

What's a catchphrase? Why's it funny? Who is Tommy Handley anyway?

'What's a catchphrase, Mum? Why's it funny?'

'I'll tell you when it's finished.'

They waved at me to be quiet.

'Turn it up, Doreen.'

My Auntie Doreen twiddled with the knob on the wireless. Oh, there he goes again: '*I don't mind if I do*', and they both laughed even louder this time and my mum started taking him off.

'*I don't mind if I do . . . !*'

My Auntie Doreen had to take out her hanky to wipe away the tears that were rolling down her cheeks.

'Oh, stop it, Freda, you're makin' me wet myself . . .'

What's he on about now, this Tommy Handley bloke? '*Colonel Chinstrap, you're an absolute nitwit!*' and my mum and my Auntie Doreen fell about laughing.

Nitwit. That's what Reverend Dutton called me and Norbert the other day when we ran into him in the corridor. 'You are a pair of clumsy nitwits, you two.' Thank goodness his cup of tea wasn't too hot, it could have scalded him. If it'd been Melrose we'd run into it would have been more than nitwits, more like the cane from the headmaster . . . Oh no, the note! I'd forgotten all about it. I went out into the hall to get it from my coat pocket. We'd been given it at school for our parents. I was meant to give it to my mum when I got home. I went back into the kitchen. They were sitting there giggling away at Tommy Handley.

'Eeh, he's a tonic, isn't he, Doreen?'

The audience on the wireless were cheering and laughing.

'I've got nits.'

I handed my mum the note. She grabbed it. She wasn't giggling now.

'What do you mean, you've got nits? Who said?'

'Nit-nurse. She came to our school today.'

Next thing she was up on her feet and going through my hair.

'Oh my God, look at this, Doreen, he's riddled!'

'*Can I do you now, sir?*' the lady on the radio was asking Tommy Handley but my mum wasn't listening; she was halfway to the front door, putting on her coat.

'Get the kettle on, Doreen. I'm going down the chemist to get some stuff.'

'At this time of night? He'll be long closed.'

'Well, he'll have to open up then, won't he? It's an emergency. He can't go to bed with nits.'

She'd come back with two lots of 'stuff'. Special nit shampoo and special nit lotion.

'One and nine this lot cost! Come on, get that shirt off.'

She'd sat me at the kitchen sink while my Auntie Doreen had got the saucepans of hot water ready. Nit shampoo smells horrible, like carbolic soap only worse.

'Doreen, put another kettle on, will you? It says you have to do it twice.'

Another shampoo and then the special lotion. I'd had to sit there with it on for ages while my mum had kept going on about missing Tommy Handley.

'It's not his fault, Freda. He can't help getting nits.'

Then it had started to sting, the nit lotion.

'No, he's most likely caught them off that Norbert Lightowler. They're a grubby lot, that family.'

It had got worse, my head was burning.

'I don't like this, Mum. It's burning me.'

'Good, that means it's working . . .'

'Ow! Ooh! Mum, stop, please, you're hurting me . . .'

The nit lotion was bad but this was worse. She was pulling this little steel comb through my hair and it hurt like anything.

'Please, Mum, I don't like it . . . please . . .'

If I hadn't made her miss Tommy Handley I think she might have been a bit more gentle.

'You couldn't have given me that note as soon as you got back from school, could you? No, you had to wait till *ITMA* was on, didn't you?'

4

I don't know if it was the smelly nit shampoo or the stinging nit lotion or my mum dragging the metal comb through my hair, but I didn't feel very well.

'You know how much your Auntie Doreen and me look forward to it.'

I started to feel a bit dizzy.

'He's the bright spot in the week for me. I don't reckon we'd have got through the war without Tommy Handley, eh, Doreen? Him and Mr Churchill.'

'And Vera Lynn.'

'Oh yes, and Vera Lynn.'

It was getting worse. The room was going round now. Everything was spinning. What was happening? I don't feel well. I wish my mum would stop pulling that comb through my hair, she's hurting me. I feel funny. What are they doing now? They're singing. Why are they singing? Why are my mum and my Auntie Doreen singing?

'We'll meet again, don't know whe-ere, don't know whe-en . . .'
'We'll meet again, don't know whe-ere, don't know whe-en . . .'

Their voices seem miles away.

'But I kno-oow we'll meet agai-in . . .'
'But I kno-oow we'll meet agai-in . . .'

I'm fainting – that's what it is. I'm fainting. Now I know

what it feels like. When Keith Hopwood had fainted in the playground I'd asked him what it had felt like and he'd said he couldn't remember much except that everything had been going round and round and everybody's voices seemed to be a long way away. That's what's happening to me. Mum! Auntie Doreen! I can see them and they're going round and round. I'm fainting! I can hear them, they're singing and they're miles away. I'm fainting!

'Some sunny . . .'
'Some sunny . . .'

I was lying on the sofa and and my mum was dabbing my face with a damp tea towel, muttering to herself.

'Come on, Doreen, where've you got to? Hurry up, hurry up.'

My hair was still wet with the nit lotion but she'd stopped combing it, thank goodness.

'What happened? What's going on?'

'You passed out, love, you scared the life out of me. Your Auntie Doreen's gone to fetch Dr Jowett.'

The one good thing about fainting is that everybody makes a fuss of you. After Keith had passed out the care-taker had carried him to the staffroom and while they'd waited for the doctor Mrs Jolliffe had given him a cup of sweet tea and some chocolate digestives. With me it was a mug of Ovaltine and a Blue Riband on the sofa while we waited for Dr Jowett.

'Have you any more Blue Ribands, Mum?'

'I haven't, love. And I won't be getting any more till I get my new ration book.'

Why does all the good stuff have to be on rationing? I bet nit shampoo and nit lotion's not on rationing.

'Will I be going to school tomorrer?'

That'd be great if I could get off school, worth fainting for. Double maths on a Friday, I hate maths. And scripture with Reverend Dutton. Borin'.

'Let's wait and see what Dr Jowett says.'

And Latin with Bleasdale. Then we have English with Melrose. Worst day of the week, Friday. English with Melrose! Oh no! I haven't done his homework! I was going to do it after *ITMA*, wasn't I?

'I don't think I should, Mum. I might faint again. You never know.'

'We'll leave it to Dr Jowett, eh?'

'Breathe in. Out. In again.'

It wasn't Dr Jowett; it was a lady doctor who was standing in for him 'cos he was at a conference or something. I'd heard my Auntie Doreen tell me mum after she'd gone to get something from her car.

'Out. In. Cough.'

I breathed out and I breathed in and I coughed like she told me. The thing she was using to listen to my chest was freezing cold and it made me laugh.

'It's a relief to see him smiling, doctor. He looked as white as a sheet twenty minutes ago.'

The lady doctor wrote something on a brown card.

'Can I stay off school tomorrer?'

She carried on writing.

'I don't see why—'

Oh great. No maths, no Latin, no scripture, no Melrose . . .

'—you shouldn't go.'

What? No, no. 'I don't see why *not*.' That's what I thought you were going to say. That's what you're supposed to say.

'But I haven't done my English homework 'cos of all this.'

'I'll give your mother a note to give to your teacher.'

She smiled and gave me a friendly pat on my head. My hair was still sticky.

'I've got nits.'

My mum gave me one of her looks.

'Outbreak at school, doctor. You know what it's like.'

'Of course.'

'Maybe that's what made him faint. It's strong stuff, that lotion.'

She shone a light in my eyes.

'Unlikely.'

She looked down my throat and in my ears. After that she put a strap round my arm and pumped on this rubber thing. It didn't hurt, just felt a bit funny. She wrote on the brown card again.

'He's small for his age.'

'Always has been, doctor.'

'But he's particularly small. And he's anaemic. I'd say he's undernourished.'

I didn't know what she was talking about but my mum didn't like it. She sat up straight and folded her arms and the red blotch started coming up on her neck. She always gets it when she's upset.

'There's only so many coupons in a ration book, doctor. I do my best. It's weeks since this house has seen fresh fruit and vegetables. He gets his cod liver oil and his orange juice and his Virol. I do what I can. That nit lotion and shampoo cost one and nine. It's not easy on your own, you know.'

The doctor wrote on the brown card again.

'Excuse me, I'm just going to get something from the car.'

My mum watched her go. The blotch on her neck was getting redder.

'Who's she? Where's Dr Jowett?'

'She's standing in for him while he's at a conference. She's very nice. Came straight away.'

'Very nice? I don't think it's very nice to be told I'm neglecting my own son. I'll give her undernourished!'

'Give over, Freda, she said nothing of the sort. Don't be so bloody soft, we've just had a war. We're all undernourished with this bloody rationing!'

I don't know who was more shocked, me or my mum. You never hear my Auntie Doreen swear. You'd have thought it was my fault, the way my mum turned on me.

'And why did you have to tell her you've got nits? Showing me up like that.'

My Auntie Doreen was just about to have another go when we heard the lady doctor coming back.

'I was going to write a prescription for a course of iron tablets but I remembered I'd got some in the car.'

She gave my mum a brown bottle.

'I don't mind paying, doctor.'

The doctor didn't say anything, just smiled.

'Now, I'll tell you what he really needs – a couple of weeks by the sea.'

My mum looked at her, then burst out laughing.

'A couple of weeks by the sea! Yes, that's what we all need, eh, Doreen?'

The lady doctor put everything back in her black bag.

'It can be arranged. And it won't cost a penny. I'll talk to Dr Jowett.'

I looked at my mum and my Auntie Doreen.

'He'll probably have to take time off school, but it would do him the world of good.'

A couple of weeks by the sea! Free! Time off school! Sounded good to me.

DEAR MUM,
I HATE IT HERE. WHY DID DOCTOR JOWETT
AND THAT LADY DOCTOR SEND ME TO THIS
HORRABLE PLACE? I WANT TO COME HOME. YOU
PROMISED THAT IF I DID NOT LIKE IT HERE
YOU WOULD COME AND FETCH ME. I DON'T LIKE

IT SO FETCH ME WHEN YOU GET THIS LETTER.
MORCAMBE IS ONLY TWO HOURS AWAY. YOU
SAID SO YOURSELF . . .

Yeah, it sounded good 'cos I thought she'd meant all of us. Me, my mum and my Auntie Doreen. Nobody'd said I'd be going on my own. I wouldn't have gone, would I? My mum never told me. Dr Jowett never told me. He was in the kitchen talking to her when I got home from school on the Friday.

'Talk of the devil, here he is. Do you want to tell him the good news, Dr Jowett?'

He had a big smile on his face when he told me. I couldn't believe it. It turned out that because I'm small for me age and all that other stuff the lady doctor had talked to my mum about, we got to go to Morecambe for free. The council paid.

'And my mum doesn't have to pay anything?'

Dr Jowett pulled my bottom lids down and looked in my eyes, like the lady doctor did the night before.

'Not a penny. It's a special scheme paid for by the council to give young folk like yourself a bit of sea air. Build you up. You'll come back six inches taller. Now, do you want to go for two weeks or one?'

Why would I want to go for one week when we could go for two? I looked at my mum.

'It's up to you, love . . .'

If she'd have said, '*It's up to you, love, 'cos you're the one* going, not me, I'm not comin', neither's your Auntie Doreen, it's just you on your own,' I'd never have said it.

'It's up to you, love – do you want to go for two weeks?'

It'd be stupid not to go for two weeks when it's free. So I said it. Just like the man on the wireless.

'I don't mind if I do!'

We all laughed.

DEAR MUM,
PLEASE COME FOR ME. I CAN'T STAY HERE. I
HATE IT. YOU PROMISED YOU WOULD FETCH ME
IF I DIDN'T LIKE IT . . .

After Dr Jowett had gone we sat at the kitchen table and looked at the leaflet he'd left for us. It looked lovely. I listened while my mum read it out.

'"*Craig House – a home from home. Overlooking Morecambe Bay, Craig House gives poor children the opportunity to get away from the grime of the city to the fresh air of the seaside . . .*" Sounds lovely, doesn't it?'

'Yeah. What does that bit mean?'

'What bit?'

'That bit about poor children. Do you have to be poor to go there?'

She looked at me.

'Well, it is for people what can't afford it, like us. That's why we're getting it for free.'

'Oh . . .'

We both looked at the leaflet again.

'There's nothing wrong with it, love. It's our right. Dr Jowett says. I mean, it'd be daft to give free holidays to them that can pay for it.'

Yeah, that was true.

'I suppose so.'

MUM, WHY HAVEN'T YOU COLLECTED ME FROM HERE? YOU PROMISED. YOU SAID IF I WAS UNHAPY YOU WOULD TAKE ME HOME. PLEASE COME AS SOON AS YOU GET THIS. PLEASE . . .

It just never crossed my mind that I was going on my own. I had no idea. It wasn't till the Sunday night, when my mum was packing my suitcase, that I found out.

'Now, I've put you two swimming costumes in so when one's wet you can wear the other, and you've plenty of underpants and vests . . .'

Even then it didn't dawn on me. I'd felt good having my own suitcase, grown up. When we'd gone to Bridlington she packed all our things together but we'd only gone for two days. This time we were going for two weeks. I thought that's why she was giving me my own suitcase.

'. . . and I'm putting in a few sweets for you, some Nuttall's Mintoes, some fruit pastilles and a bar of chocolate. You can thank your Auntie Doreen for them, she saved up her coupons.'

I still didn't realise.

'Well, we can share them, can't we?'

13

'No, these are all for you.'

I thought she was just being nice, getting in the holiday mood.

'Now, this is important. I'm giving you these to take –' she held up some envelopes – 'they're all stamped and addressed so you can write to me every day if you like . . .'

You what? What are you talking about? What is she talking about?

'You don't have to write every day, I'm only joking, but I would like to get the occasional letter. They're here, under your pants.'

What was she talking about? When it all came out that I'd thought they were coming with me, she'd looked at me like I'd gone off my head.

'But why? What on earth made you think me and your Auntie Doreen were coming?'

''Cos you said.'

'I never. I never said we were all going.'

She was lying. She did.

'You did. When the lady doctor said I needed a holiday, you told her that's what we *all* needed, a couple of weeks by the sea. You ask Auntie Doreen.'

I'd cried and told her that I wasn't going to go and she said I had to, it'd all been arranged, I'd show her up in front of Dr Jowett if I didn't go. And it wouldn't be fair if I didn't go, it would be a wasted space that some other child could have used.

'It's not fair on me, 'cos if I'd known I wouldn't have said I'd go for two weeks. I wouldn't have gone for *one*

14

week. I'm not goin', I don't want to go. Please don't make me go . . .'

I cried, I begged, I shut myself in my bedroom. I wasn't going to go, I wasn't.

'I'm not goin'. You can't force me.'

She couldn't force me.

'Listen, love, if you don't like it, if you're really unhappy, I'll get straight on the train and bring you home.'

'Promise?'

'It's less than two hours away.'

'Promise?'

''Course.'

'Promise!'

'I promise.'

My mum let me sleep in her bed that night 'cos I couldn't stop crying.

'Come on, love, go to sleep, we've got to be at Great Albert Street at eight o'clock for your coach.'

'You promise to fetch me if I don't like it?'

'But you will like it and it'll do you good.'

'You promise, don't you?'

'As soon as I get your letter.'

And I fell asleep.

Craig House holiday home
far far away,
Where us poor children go
for a holiday.
Oh, how we run like hell

15

when we hear the dinner bell,
far far away.

DEAR MUM,
I HATE IT HERE. WHY DID DOCTOR JOWETT
AND THAT LADY DOCTOR SEND ME TO THIS
HORRABLE PLACE? I WANT TO COME HOME. YOU
PROMISED THAT IF I DID NOT LIKE IT HERE
YOU WOULD COME AND FETCH ME. I DON'T LIKE
IT SO FETCH ME WHEN YOU GET THIS LETTER.
MORCAMBE IS ONLY TWO HOURS AWAY. YOU
SAID SO YOURSELF . . .

That was the first letter.

DEAR MUM,
PLEASE COME FOR ME. I CAN'T STAY HERE. I
HATE IT. YOU PROMISED YOU WOULD FETCH ME
IF I DIDN'T LIKE IT . . .

That was the second letter.

MUM, WHY HAVEN'T YOU COME . . .?

Why hadn't she come for me? She'd promised . . .

THIS IS THE THIRD TIME I'VE WRITTEN . . .

We'd been told we had to be outside the medical clinic in

16

Great Albert Street at eight o'clock for the coach. We were going to be weighed before we went and they'd weigh us when we got back to see how much we'd put on. My Auntie Doreen came with us, and even on the bus to town I made them both promise again. We turned into Great Albert Street at five to and I could see lots of kids waiting on the pavement with their mums and dads and grandmas and grandads. There was no coach. Good, maybe it had broken down and I wouldn't have to go. My mum carried my suitcase and we walked up the road towards them. A big cheer went up as the coach came round the corner at the top end of the street.

When we got closer I saw that some of the kids looked funny. One lad had no hair, another was bandy. There was a girl with these iron things on her legs. My mum gave me a sharp tap 'cos I was staring at the bald lad.

'What's wrong with him, Mum?'

'Alopecia, most likely.'

'What's that?'

'It's when your hair drops out. Poor lad.'

'Do you get it from nits?'

'Don't be daft.'

My Auntie Doreen told me it can be caused by stress or shock.

'Do you remember that teacher we had at primary, Freda, Mrs Theobold? She lost all her hair when her husband got knocked down by a tram.'

My mum shook her head.

'Oh, you do. She had to wear a wig.'

17

'I don't.'

We stood outside the medical clinic next to a woman with a ginger-headed lad. His face looked ever so sore, all flaky and red. My mum gave me another sharp tap. The woman got a packet of Woodbines out of her handbag.

'Oh, don't worry, missus, he's used to young 'uns staring, aren't you, Eric?'

Eric nodded while she lit a cigarette.

'Eczema. Not infectious, love. Had it all his life, haven't you, Eric?'

He nodded again. My Auntie Doreen smiled at him.

'Two weeks in Morecambe'll be just what he needs, eh?'

The woman coughed as she blew the smoke out.

'Don't know about him but it'll do me a power of good. I need a break, I can tell you.'

Just then a man came out of the clinic and shouted that we all had to go inside to be weighed.

'Parents, foster parents and guardians – wait out here while the luggage is put on the charabanc. The children will return as soon as they've been weighed and measured.'

Eric's mum took another puff on her cigarette.

'I don't know why they bother. Last year he came back weighing less than when he went, didn't you, Eric?'

Eric nodded again.

'And I swear he was half an inch shorter. Off you go then.'

I followed him into the clinic, where the man was telling everybody to go up the main stairs and turn left.

'Have you been before then, to Craig House?'

He'd been for the last two years.

'What's it like?'

'S'all right. Better than being at home.'

At the top of the stairs we followed the ones in front into a big room where we were told to take our clothes off. We had to strip down to our vests and pants and sit on a stool until we heard our name called out. There were four weighing scales, with a number above each one. I sat next to Eric. He didn't have a vest on and his pants had holes in them and whatever his mum had said he had, he had it all over, he looked horrible. I couldn't help staring. He didn't seem bothered though. He just sat there, scratching, staring at the floor.

'Eric Braithwaite, weighing scale three! Eric Braithwaite, weighing scale three!'

He didn't say anything, just wandered off to be weighed and measured. I sat waiting for my name to be called out. The girl with iron things on her legs was on the other side of the room. Her mum and dad had been allowed to come in and were taking the iron things off and helping her get undressed.

'Margaret Donoghue, weighing scale one! Margaret Donoghue, weighing scale one!'

That was her. Her dad had to carry her, she couldn't walk without her iron things. Eric came back, put his clothes back on and wandered off. He didn't speak, didn't say a word. They were going in alphabetical order so I had to wait quite a long time before I heard my name. When I

19

did I had to go to weighing scale number four. A lady in a white coat told me to get on.

'There's nothing of you, is there? A couple of weeks at Craig House'll do you no harm.'

She wrote my weight down in a book.

'Now, let's see how small you are.'

Couple of weeks? I wasn't going to be there a couple of weeks. Not if I didn't like it. And I *wasn't* going to like it, I knew that much.

'Right, get dressed and go back to your mum and dad.'

'I haven't got a dad.'

'Ellis Roper! Weighing scale number four! Ellis Roper, weighing scale number four! You what, dear?'

'I haven't got a dad.'

'Well, go back to whoever brought you. Ellis Roper, please! Weighing scale number four!'

Craig House holiday home
far far away,
Where us poor children go
for a holiday.
Oh, how we run like hell
when we hear the dinner bell,
far far away.

We were on our way to Morecambe and those that had been before were singing this stupid song. I was in an aisle seat next to the bald lad. He was singing, so I knew it wasn't his first time. I'd wanted to get by the window so I could wave goodbye to my mum and my Auntie Doreen but by the time I'd been weighed and measured I was too late. Eric was next to me on the other side of the aisle. He wasn't singing, just sitting there staring into space. Behind me a girl was crying. She hadn't wanted to go. The driver and the man from the clinic had had to drag her away from her mum and force her on to the coach. Her mum had run off up the street crying, with her dad following. They didn't even wave her off. My mum had had to get her hanky out 'cos she had tears in her eyes.

'Don't forget to write – your envelopes are in your suit-case under your pants.'

'Course I wouldn't forget. I had it all planned. I was going to write as soon as I got there and post it straight away. My mum'd get the letter on the Tuesday morning, get on the train like she'd promised and I'd be home for Tuesday night. That's why I wasn't crying like the girl behind me. I was only going to be away for one day, wasn't I?

I was looking at the bald lad when he turned round. I made out I'd been looking out of the window but I reckon he knew I'd been staring at him.

'I've got alopecia.'

He smiled. He didn't have any eyebrows neither.

'Oh . . .' I didn't know what to say. 'How long have you had it?'

'A few years. I went to bed one night and when I woke up it was lyin' there on my pillow. My hair.'

I felt sick.

'It just fell out?'

'Yeah. It was after my gran got a telegram tellin' her that my dad had been killed at Dunkirk. I live with my gran. My mum died when I was two.'

I told him that I lived with my mum and that my auntie lived two streets away.

'Did *your* dad die in the war?'

'I don't know. Don't think so. I've never known him.'

He was all right, Paul, I quite liked him. He told me it wasn't too bad at Craig House. This was his third year running.

'It's not bad. They've got table tennis and football and they take you on the beach. And you get a cooked breakfast every mornin'. You get a stick of rock when you leave. It's all right.'

Maybe it wouldn't be as bad as I thought. Maybe I'd like it. Maybe I wouldn't want to go home.

MUM, WHY HAVEN'T YOU COME? THIS IS THE
THIRD TIME I'VE WRITTEN. I HATE IT HERE . . .

'Look – the sea!'

It was one of the big lads at the back shouting, the one who'd started the singing. Everybody leaned over to our side of the coach to get a look. Eric didn't; he just sat there, staring and scratching his face. For some of them, like the girl behind me, it was the first time they'd seen the sea. She was all right now, laughing and giggling and talking away to the girl next to her. The man from the clinic stood up at the front and told us all to sit down.

'We'll be arriving at Craig House in five minutes. Do not leave this coach until I give the word. When you hear your name you will alight the charabanc, retrieve your luggage, which will be on the pavement, and proceed to the home.'

The coach pulled round a corner and there it was. There was a big sign by the entrance:

CRAIG HOUSE

And underneath it said:

Poor Children's Holiday Home

We all stood in the entrance hall holding our suitcases while our names were called out and we were told which dormitory we were in. There was this smell and it was horrible. Like school dinners and hospitals mixed together. It made me feel sick. There were four dormitories, two for the girls and two for the boys. I was in General Montgomery dormitory and I followed my group. We were going up the stairs when I saw it. A post box. I'd been worried that they wouldn't let me out to find a post box and there was one right here in the entrance hall. I could post my letter here in Craig House. It wasn't like a normal post box that you see in the street; it was made of cardboard and painted red and the hole where you put the letters was a smiling mouth.

I wasn't able to write it until late that afternoon.

When we'd been given our bed we were taken to the showers and scrubbed clean by these ladies and had our hair washed with nit shampoo. I tried to tell my lady that my mum had already done it but she didn't want to know.

'Best be safe than sorry, young man.'

Then we were given a Craig House uniform (they'd taken our clothes off to be washed). Shirt, short trousers, jumper. They even gave us pyjamas. And on everything was a ribbon that said 'Poor Children's Holiday Home'. You couldn't take it off, it was sewn on.

At last, after our tea, I'd been able to write my letter. I licked the envelope, made sure it was stuck down properly and ran down the main stairs.

'Walk, lad. Don't run. Nobody runs at Craig House.'

That was the warden. I walked across the entrance hall to the post box and put my letter into the smiling mouth. All I had to do now was wait for my mum to come and fetch me.

MUM, WHY HAVEN'T YOU COME? THIS IS THE THIRD TIME I'VE WRITTEN. I HATE IT HERE. THERE ARE TWO LADS THAT BULLY ME. THEY HAVE TAKEN ALL MY SWEETS . . .

I hated it. I hated it. I couldn't see why Paul thought it was all right. Or Eric. Not that I saw much of them. They were in General Alanbrooke dormitory. I think I was the youngest in General Montgomery. I was the smallest anyway – they were all bigger than me. My bed was between the two who had started the singing at the back of the coach and at night after the matron had switched off the lights they said things to frighten me and they made these scary noises. I thought they might be nicer to me if I gave them each a Nuttall's Mintoe. When they saw all my other sweets in my suitcase they made me hand them all over. I hated them. I dreaded going to bed 'cos I was so scared. I was too scared to go to sleep. I was too scared to get up and go to the lavatory. Then in the morning I'd find I'd wet the bed and I'd get told off in front of everybody and have to stand out on the balcony as a punishment.

And I hated my mum. She'd broken her promise. You can never trust grown-ups.

DEAR MUM, YOU PROMISED. YOU SAID IF I WAS
UNHAPY YOU WOULD TAKE ME HOME. YOU
HAVEN'T COME. I AM SO UNHAPY. PLEASE FETCH
ME AS SOON AS YOU GET THIS . . .

I licked the envelope and stuck it down like I'd done with all the others. I walked downstairs to the entrance hall and went over to the post box. I was just about to put it in the smiling mouth when I heard Eric.

'What you doin'?'

'Sendin' a letter to my mum.'

Eric laughed. Well, it wasn't a laugh, more of a snort.

'It's not a proper post box. They don't post 'em.'

I looked at him.

'They say they post 'em but they don't. They don't want us pestering 'em at home.'

I still had the letter in my hand.

'I won't bother then.'

I tore it up and went back to the dormitory. The second week went quicker and I didn't wet the bed.

'You didn't send one letter, you little monkey.'

My mum wasn't really cross that I hadn't written.

'It shows he had a good time, doesn't it, Doreen? See, I told you you'd like it.'

She was annoyed at how much weight I'd lost.

THE MAJOR

I should never have told my mum. I wish I'd never mentioned it. I felt stupid standing in my vest and underpants in the middle of the kitchen with a curly wig stuck on my head.

'Stand up straight while I fix your hair and keep still for goodness sake.'

You could hardly tell what she was saying 'cos she was holding these hairgrips in her mouth. She got hold of the wig and pulled the back of it.

'Doreen, just hold the front in place while I stick these bobby pins in, will you?'

Bobby pins, that's what they're called, not hairgrips, she had about six of them between her lips.

'Ow! That hurts!'

'Oh stop mithering, you'll thank me when you win, keep still.'

And she stuck another one in, right into my neck.

'Freda, you're going to swallow one of those if you keep talking, give them to me and I'll pass them to you as and when.'

My mum spat the bobby pins out into my Auntie Doreen's hand, took one and stuck it in the wig.

'Ow!'

'Stand still.'

'I don't want to go.'

'Don't start that again, not now, not after the effort me and your Auntie Doreen have put in.'

I wish I'd never mentioned it. I should never have told her about the fancy-dress competition.

'Happy Birthday to you
Happy Birthday to you
Happy Birthday dear . . .'

We all took a deep breath: '*David – Raymond – Christine . . .*'

The cinema manager held his hand over their heads and shouted their names into his microphone as he walked behind them on the stage. We all sang along, trying to keep up with him.

'Trevor – Margaret – and another David!'

'. . . *Trevor – Margaret – and Da-v-id . . .*'

Except Norbert sang '*and another Da-v-id*'.

'*Happy Birthday to you!*'

We tried to make the final 'you' last as long as we could, we do it every week, and Norbert went on longer than the rest of us and slid off his seat on to the floor, still singing and running out of breath. One of the usherettes pointed at him and pointed to the door.

'Any more and you're out. I've been watching you, lad.'

Uncle Derek, that's the cinema manager, gave them

their ABC Minors birthday cards and we all clapped while they went back to their seats. I'd gone up on the stage the week of my birthday and it's not just a birthday card you get, it's a pass that gets you in for free the next week with pictures of film stars on it, like Lassie and Laurel and Hardy and Roy Rogers and that girl in *The Wizard of Oz* – I didn't like that film, it gave me nightmares – and Mickey Mouse and Donald Duck, but best of all it says: 'PLEASE ADMIT BEARER AS MY GUEST' and it's signed by Uncle Derek.

The usherette was still watching Norbert. He got up off the floor and scrambled back into his seat.

'I haven't done nothin', missus. Honest. I were just singin'.'

'*And* messin' about. Don't think I don't remember you, lad, I do. I ejected you two weeks back for throwin' Butterkist.'

She went off to separate two lads near the front who were fighting. She got hold of them both by their collars and marched them up the aisle.

'If she chucks me out, you'll have to let me back in at the side door when the lights go down.'

'Me?'

I wasn't going to risk getting thrown out just to let him in again.

'I'll give you three sherbet lemons.'

I gave him the sort of look my mum gives me when I've said something stupid.

'Get lost, ask Keith.'

'He's gone to the lav.'

'Well, make sure he's back before you get chucked out.'

That's how he'd got in without paying earlier on. It's how he gets in every week, he never pays to go to the Saturday morning matinee, doesn't Norbert. He goes round the back of the picture house, up Shadwell Street, and gets Keith Hopwood to push down the bar on the inside of the side door. He gives Keith some of his sweets for doing it. Mind you, he never pays for them neither, he nicks them. We all do, every Saturday, me, Tony, Norbert and Keith Hopwood. But we're not going to any more, Keith, Tony and me anyway, we'd decided that morning.

'Now, boys and girls, we've got a wonderful selection of films for you today starting with the Bowery Boys . . .'

Everybody cheered and there were the usual boos.

'A Mighty Mouse cartoon . . .'

More cheers and boos.

'Shh, shush, listen to Uncle Derek now . . .'

We meet by the park gates every Saturday at around half past nine to get the bus into town, but we always go across the road to Major Creswell's first to buy our sweets. Well, to steal them. We pay for some, a few. But even if we had the money we couldn't buy more than a few, 'cos we never have enough coupons. Why do they have to have sweets on rationing anyway? It's not fair.

'And – the final episode of *Flash Gordon*!'

No boos this time. Cheering and shouting and whistling and everybody stamping their feet. It was deafening.

30

'And the big picture today, boys and girls . . .'

It's easy nicking sweets and stuff in the Major's shop, always has been, ever since he took it over from old Mrs Jesmond last year. Norbert always asks for something off the top shelf and while the Major's moving the ladder and going up it, Norbert just helps himself to whatever he wants. One time he even went round the counter and pretended to serve us.

'The big picture today, girls and boys . . . Shush, now listen, don't you want to know . . . ?'

'YES!'

Everybody shouted as loud as they could.

'Yes what?'

'YES, PLEASE!'

'The big picture is . . .'

I feel a bit sorry for the Major but I still do it with all the others. I never take as much as Norbert. The week before last he'd come out with a whole box of pear drops. I just take a few of the loose things that the Major has on the counter. A couple of Poor Bens or a Vimto bar or maybe a few sherbet lemons, hardly anything. You can't really call it stealing.

'The big picture is – *Tarzan*!'

Cheers, shouts, boos, stamping. We all went mad, specially Norbert. He stood on his seat and did Tarzan's jungle call. He was lucky the usherette didn't see him, she was too busy trying to catch these lads who were running up and down the aisle. I think they were from St Cuthbert's. They always go a bit mad, St Cuthbert's lads.

Anyway, I'm not going to do it any more, the stealing. None of us are – except Norbert. We'd decided to stop when the Major had asked us to look after the shop while he went upstairs to check on Mrs Creswell. He'd come down the ladder just as we'd put the stuff in our pockets. I was lucky he didn't catch me, I'd dropped a liquorice stick on the floor and got it away just in time.

'Listen, chaps, would you do me a favour? Would you keep an eye on things down here for a couple of minutes? I just want to pop upstairs and check on the little lady. The old girl's having one of her bad days, I'm afraid . . .'

The Major's wife is an invalid, she has to stay upstairs above the shop. We never see her, I think she's in bed most of the time. We don't even know what she looks like.

'I thought I'd make her a quick cup of tea. Have you got the time?'

Norbert's eyes lit up.

'Yeah, you're all right, Major Creswell, we'll watch the shop.'

'I don't want to make you late for your Saturday matinee.'

Norbert looked at us.

'No, it doesn't start till half past ten, Major, we've got tons of time, haven't we, lads?'

We all mumbled that we had plenty of time. We knew what he was going to do. And I knew what *I* was going to do.

'Thanks a lot, chaps, won't be long. Much appreciated.'

We watched him go into the back of the shop and heard him go upstairs.

'Are you all right, dear? Thought you might like a cup of tea, old thing. A bunch of my regular customers are very kindly looking after the shop . . .'

We looked at each other. Norbert had this stupid grin on his face.

'Bloomin' hummer, we can take what we like!'

Uncle Derek was 'shushing' into the microphone.

'Now, before we start the first film, I've got an important announcement to make . . .'

More boos. We all stamped our feet. Norbert looked round to check where the usherette was and stood on his seat to boo.

'No, no, listen, boys and girls, this is something very exciting, you'll like this, listen. Next week we're going to have, up here on the stage, a film-star fancy-dress competition . . . !'

Tons of boos.

'You have to dress up as your favourite film star and the first prize, courtesy of the Directors and Management of Associated British Cinemas – listen now, it's something special, quiet now – first prize will be a *year's* free pass to the ABC Saturday Morning Matinee . . .'

Stamping feet, cheering, whistling. I thought the roof was going to come down.

'Second prize, a free pass for six months and third prize,

a three-month pass. I told you it was special. Now remember, you do have to dress up as a film star . . .'

Norbert was shouting at me but I couldn't tell what he was saying with all the noise.

'Y'what?'

'Free pass for a year! Bloomin' hummer, I'm goin' in for that.'

I couldn't understand what he was so excited about, he gets in free anyway, every week.

'And now it's showtime!'

The lights started to go down and the curtain turned red, then deep red and went up slowly. The music started.

'We are the boys and girls well known
As Minors of the ABC,
And every Saturday we line up
To see the films we like
And shout with glee . . .'

Norbert went round to the back of the counter. He still had his stupid grin on his face.

'You lot listen out for him. What do you want? Liquorice cuttings? Oh look, sherbet lemons.'

I got hold of his jumper and pulled him back.

'No! He's asked us to look after the shop.'

Norbert pulled himself free and took a handful of the sherbet lemons.

'Sod off, I'm not missin' a chance like this.'

34

He put the sherbet lemons into one of his trouser pockets and grabbed another handful.

'Well, I'm not takin' anything. In fact, I'm putting my stuff back.'

I got the liquorice stick that I'd pinched out of my pocket and put it back in the box on the counter. Norbert was still taking stuff.

'Keith, listen out for him.'

'No, I'm p-p-putting mine b-back an' all.'

Keith emptied his pockets. So did Tony.

'So am I.'

Norbert stopped for a minute and looked at us.

'You're soft, you lot!'

He grabbed some dolly mixtures and ran out.

'I'll see you down there.'

He slammed the door shut. A second later it opened again and he came back in. I thought maybe he'd changed his mind and was going to put the sweets back, but he didn't. He went over to the lolly cabinet, took a Koola Fruta and ran out again. Every time he went in and out the shop doorbell rang. The Major thought it was customers, we heard him coming back down the stairs.

'Sounds like it's getting quite busy down there, dear, better go and relieve the troops. I'll pop up again later, old thing, when it quietens down.'

Tony, Keith and me waited for the Major to come back into the shop. He looked surprised.

'Oh! I thought I heard a couple of customers come in.'

I waited for the others to say something but they didn't.

'No, Major Creswell, it was Norbert . . . he was worried about bein' late so he went. He came back to . . . er . . . borrow some money for the bus.'

The Major went round the counter.

'Thanks for holding the fort, chaps. Here you are, a little something for keeping an eye on things down here.'

He held up three bars of Five Boys chocolate. We looked at each other, we didn't know what to do. We hadn't stolen any sweets now so I reckoned it was all right. I took one.

'Thanks, Major Creswell.'

Keith and Tony took theirs.

'Yes, th-thanks, M-Major.'

'Ta, Major.'

He held out another bar.

'And one for your chum.'

We stopped at the door. Nobody wanted to take it but I didn't have any choice, the Major threw it over and I was the one to catch it.

'Thank you, Major Creswell, we'll give it to him when we see him.'

As soon as we got to the bus stop we divided it into three and ate it on the way to the matinee.

'We love to laugh and have a sing-song,
Such a happy crowd are we.
We're all pals together,
The Minors of the ABC!'

*

'And Mum, listen to this, first prize is a free pass for a year!'

As soon as I'd got home from the pictures, I'd told her about the fancy-dress competition.

'You have to dress as a film star, what shall I go as?'

'Ow!'

'Stand still.'

'I don't want to go.'

'Don't start that again, not now, not after the effort me and your Auntie Doreen have put in.'

I wish I'd never mentioned it. I should never have told her about the fancy-dress competition.

'What do you think, Mum? Charlie Chaplin?'

She was laying the table.

'We'll ask your Auntie Doreen when she gets here, she'll have some ideas.'

I love Saturdays. Matinee in the morning, then usually we have fish and chips for dinner, my Auntie Doreen gets them fresh from Pearson's on her way over.

'What do you think I should go as, Auntie Doreen?'

I shook some more vinegar over my fish and chips. My mum snatched the bottle out of my hand.

'Don't drown them like that, you'll spoil your dinner. What do you think, Doreen, Charlie Chaplin?'

My Auntie Doreen put some more vinegar on her fish and chips. She's like me, she has tons of it. My mum doesn't tell her she's spoiling her dinner.

'No, they'll be ten a penny, Charlie Chaplins. They'll all be going as Charlie Chaplin or Roy Rogers. We'll have to think of something different if he wants to win.'

She did.

'Shirley Temple? She's a girl, Auntie Doreen!'

We were on our way home from church on the Sunday and my Auntie Doreen was telling my mum her idea about me entering the fancy-dress competition as Shirley Temple. She had this big smile on her face.

'It just came to me, Freda, right in the middle of the vicar's sermon . . .'

'Auntie Doreen, I don't want to go as a girl!'

She wasn't listening. Neither of them were.

'You know when he was talking about us all being just ships that pass in the night, that song Shirley Temple sings came into my head you know, out of the blue . . .'

She started singing:

'On the good ship Lollipop,
It's a sweet trip to a candy shop . . .'

Then my mum joined in.

'Where the bon-bons pla-ay,
On the sunny beach of Peppermint Ba-ay . . .'

They both fell about laughing.

'It's a good idea, Doreen, there won't be any other lads going as Shirley Temple.'

I didn't want to go as a girl.

'Mum, I don't think I want to go as a girl.'

'Exactly, Freda, he's bound to win.'

I didn't want to go as a girl.

'But I don't want to go as a girl.'

They didn't hear me, they were too busy talking about what I was going to wear. My mum said she'd get me a curly blonde wig and my Auntie Doreen said she'd make me a dress with bows on.

'I've got some lovely gingham material, it'll be perfect . . .'

'I don't think I want to go as Shirley Temple, Mum . . .'

'And I'll make him a couple of gingham bows to go in his hair.'

They started singing again and skipping down the street:

'On the good ship Lollipop,
It's a night trip, into bed you hop.
And dream awa-ay,
On the good ship—'

'I'm not goin' as a bloody girl!'

'And you don't come out until I say so! I will not have you shouting and swearing at your Auntie Doreen in the

39

middle of the street like that! Specially when she's trying to help you.'

She slammed my bedroom door shut. I'd said I was sorry. Twice.

'But I've apologised, haven't I? I've said I'm sorry!'

I could hear her stamping down the stairs.

'Twice!'

I opened the door a little bit.

'All right, I'll go as Shirley Temple if you want!'

I heard her coming back. I shut it quick.

'It makes no difference to us, you can go as Chu Chin Chow for all I care! And put your dinner plate outside the door when you've finished.'

I didn't know what she was talking about. I'd never heard of Choochinchow or whoever she was talking about. She was probably a girl too.

I didn't put my plate outside the door like my mum had told me. After I'd finished my dinner I sat on my bed for a while then I took it downstairs myself.

'Sorry, Auntie Doreen, I didn't mean to shout. Thank you for your help. I'd like to go as Shirley Temple.'

'Come here.'

I went over and she gave me a big hug.

'You go as you like, love, it was just an idea, something different.'

I looked at my mum. I didn't want to go as a girl but I didn't want to get into more trouble.

'No, I'd like to, I think it's a *good* idea.'

My mum smiled. My Auntie Doreen gave me another hug.

'Come on, Freda, get your tape measure out, I want to make a start on his dress when I get home tonight.'

I had to stand on a chair while my Auntie Doreen got all my measurements and they sang that stupid song again.

'On the good ship Lollipop,
It's a sweet trip to a candy shop . . .'

At least I wasn't in trouble any more.

'Stand still.'

'I don't want to go.'

'Don't start that again, not now, not after the effort me and your Auntie Doreen have put in.'

I wish I'd never mentioned it. I should never have told her about the fancy-dress competition.

'Now, let's get that dress on him, Doreen, see how it looks.'

Later on, after my Auntie Doreen had gone home, my mum asked me to run round to the off-licence in Mansfield Street to get her a bag of sugar.

'Here's the ration book, don't lose it, and here's the correct money. Straight there and straight back, it'll be getting dark soon.'

'Right, Mum.'

I was pleased to be helping her, I hate it when she's cross with me.

'Hang on, love.'

She opened her purse again.

'Get yourself something from the sweet shop, there's enough coupons.'

That would have been nice but the Major's is closed on a Sunday afternoon.

'He'll be closed.'

She told me to keep the money anyway, in case I saw something in the off-licence.

'Thanks, Mum.'

It was all right this. Worth going as Shirley Temple. Maybe it *was* a good idea, maybe I'd win. Even if it were only third prize I'd get a free cinema pass for three months.

I got the bag of sugar and a Wagon Wheel for myself and I started eating it on my way home.

When I went past Major Creswell's I stopped to look in the window to see what I would have bought if he'd been open. Probably some liquorice torpedoes. Or maybe sherbet lemons – if Norbert had left any, he'd taken tons. I was pressing my face against the door, looking at the sweets inside, when it opened. I couldn't believe it. The lights were all out and the closed sign was on the door but it just swung open. It hadn't been locked properly on the inside. The bell was ringing and I was standing inside the shop. I didn't know what to do. I reckoned the Major would have heard the shop bell so I waited for him to come down.

'Major Creswell? Major Creswell?'

Nobody came. I closed the door to make the bell ring again. He still didn't come down. All I could think was that it'd been a good job it was me and not Norbert who'd been leaning against the door, he'd have nicked everything by now.

'Major . . . Major Creswell?'

Still nothing. I went to the back of the shop and called up the stairs.

'Major Creswell? Are you there? The shop door wasn't locked properly . . .'

There was a light at the top of the stairs and I could hear music playing. I didn't know what to do. It was getting dark now, I had to get home for my mum. But I had to tell the Major. I couldn't just go. I went up a few of the stairs.

'Major? Major Creswell? Mrs Creswell . . . ?'

The music was quite loud, that was probably why he hadn't heard the bell. I went up a few more stairs and called a bit louder.

'Hello? Major Creswell . . . Mrs Creswell . . . Hello?'

When I got to the top of the stairs there was a landing, and the light and the music were coming from a room at the end of a corridor. The door was only half open. I walked towards it, tapped and peeped in. Mrs Creswell was sitting in a chair with her eyes closed, listening to the music.

'Mrs Creswell?'

I thought it was funny she was smoking a pipe but it was only when she spoke that I realised.

'Oh my God, old boy, you gave me the fright of my life.'

It wasn't Mrs Creswell, it was the Major.

'How on earth did you get in, old chap?'

He was dressed up as a woman.

'Sorry . . . your shop door . . . it was open . . . you hadn't locked it properly . . . Didn't you hear me shouting?'

He got up and went over to the radiogram. He was in high heels and nylon stockings like my mum wears, a red dress and he had long hair. He took off the record he was playing.

'Ah, I was in the world of Beethoven, old chum. Didn't hear a thing. Erm . . .'

He looked at me staring. He was wearing lipstick as well. And a pearl necklace.

'Are you going in for a fancy-dress competition, Major Creswell?'

It was all I could think of. Why else would he be wearing a dress?

'Er . . . no, no, this is – was – Mrs Creswell's. One of her favourites, actually. Listen, old boy, I haven't exactly been honest with you. I'm afraid Mrs Creswell . . . died some time ago.'

What was he talking about? She was here yesterday. He'd made her a cup of tea while we looked after the shop.

'I miss her so much, I sometimes pretend she's still here, pretend to make her cups of tea, that sort of thing. I know it sounds strange but it makes me feel better. That's why I wear her favourite dress sometimes too. Makes me feel closer to her.'

It was getting late. My mum'd be worried about me.

44

'I've got to go, Major, my mum'll be wonderin' where I am.'

He thanked me for letting him know about the door and told me to help myself to anything in the shop on my way out.

'No, it's all right, Major . . .'

He didn't know we'd been helping ourselves to stuff every Saturday for the last few months, ever since he'd taken the shop over.

'I'll just get going.'

He stopped me at the top of the stairs.

'Listen, old thing, I'd rather you didn't tell anybody about this, they might not understand. They might think I'm a bit silly, you know, laugh at me behind my back. Perhaps it could be – our little secret? Eh?'

I promised that I wouldn't tell anybody. And I didn't. Not even my mum.

'Where've you been? It doesn't take that long to go to the off-licence. I was beginning to get worried.'

I told her what had happened, that the shop door had opened when I'd been looking in, that I'd had to go inside and tell the Major that he hadn't locked up properly and that he was upstairs listening to music. I told her every-thing – except that he was wearing Mrs Creswell's dress. I kept that secret, like I'd promised.

'We are the boys and girls well known
As Minors of the ABC,

*And every Saturday we line up
To see the films we like
And shout with glee . . .*

Uncle Derek was telling everybody who was entering the competition to line up by the steps on the left-hand side of the stage.

'Now, when I give the word, I want you to come up the steps, one by one, and walk slowly across the stage holding up your number. When you get to the middle, face the front so the Deputy Lord Mayor and the other judges can have a good look at you, then walk to the other side of the stage and go back to your seat. Music maestro, please!'

The ones at the front started going up the steps. Norbert, Keith and Tony hadn't bothered to enter and I could see them in their seats pointing and laughing at me in my Shirley Temple dress and wig.

Norbert was stuffing his face with sweets. I wondered where he'd stolen them from now Major Creswell's was closed. I couldn't believe the Major's shop had closed down. Norbert wasn't bothered. *I* couldn't stop thinking about it.

'Ow!'

'Stand still.'

'I don't want to go.'

'Don't start that again, not now, not after the effort me and your Auntie Doreen have put in.'

'Norbert's goin' to laugh his head off when he sees me.'

I was standing in the kitchen on a stool with my mum and my Auntie Doreen admiring me in the gingham dress. I was dreading Norbert and that lot seeing me. I'd told them that I was going as Shirley Temple, I'd thought it best, but now I was in the curly wig and the dress . . . oh hell, I was dreading it.

'He won't be laughing when you're going in for free every week.'

I didn't tell her that Norbert gets in for free every week anyway, I couldn't be bothered.

'I should have gone as Charlie Chaplin.'

My mum fiddled with my wig a bit more.

'You won't be saying that when you win. And your Auntie Doreen's right, there'll be Charlie Chaplins queuing right round the picture house.'

She picked up a carrier bag.

'Now, we'll take you down on the bus and here's your clothes for you to change into after the competition. Come on, let's get going, I'll buy you some sweets from Major Creswell's on the way.'

My Auntie Doreen got hold of her arm.

'Oh, I didn't tell you, did I? He's closed down, I went past this morning. There were police all over the place. He's been arrested.'

We both stopped at the door. He'd been arrested? The Major?

'Why Auntie Doreen? Why's he been arrested?'

She gave my mum that funny look they always do when they don't want me to hear something.

'Go and put your coat on.'

'But, Mum . . .'

'Go on, love, we'll be out in a sec.'

I went out and she shut the door. But I could still hear them whispering.

'What happened, Doreen?'

'Police caught him in town – dressed up as a woman.'

'Dressed up as a woman? That's disgusting. What's the matter with the man?'

'Seems he's done it before, lots of times. I was talking to a policeman outside the shop. They reckon he'll be going to prison.'

Going to prison? For wearing a dress? Why? I couldn't understand it.

'And I'll tell you something else – there's no Mrs Creswell. He lives there on his own.'

'Cos she died, didn't she. A long time ago. That's why he wears her dress, he misses her. That's why he pretends to make her cups of tea. But I couldn't tell them. I couldn't say anything, could I? I'd get into trouble for not saying anything last Sunday.

'Now, boys and girls, remember what Uncle Derek said – when you get to the middle, turn and face the front.'

I was standing on the steps, waiting to walk across the stage, thinking about everything that had happened. I just couldn't stop thinking about Major Creswell.

'Go on, it's your turn.'

It was the lad behind, pushing me on to the stage. He'd come as Charlie Chaplin. My Auntie Doreen had been right, Charlie Chaplins *were* ten a penny. So were Shirley Temples, there were tons of them. Uncle Derek was talking into his microphone.

'And now, boys and girls, another Shirley Temple – but a Shirley Temple with a difference. Don't forget to turn to the front and face the judges when you get to the middle.'

I started walking and there was a bit of clapping. I could hear Norbert shouting out but I couldn't tell what he was saying. I was still thinking about the Major. Why did he go into town wearing the dress? I couldn't understand.

'This Shirley Temple, boys and girls, is – and you'll never believe it – this Shirley Temple is a lad!'

Everybody cheered and whistled – and I won third prize.

When the Deputy Lord Mayor presented it to me he said, 'Here you are, young lady,' and everybody laughed. I think I laughed as well, I'm not sure. I was thinking about the Major. It wasn't fair. Here I was getting a prize for wearing a dress and he was going to prison for wearing one. It didn't seem right to me.

THE AIR-RAID SHELTER

I couldn't stop crying and I was shaking. I couldn't stop myself from shaking.

'It was Mr Churchill's fault. Him and that Mr Attlee. If it hadn't been for them, none of it would have happened. We wouldn't have had the day off. I'd have been at school . . .'

I'd never even heard of Mr Attlee before that ginger-headed lad who goes to St Bede's had stopped me in the park one afternoon on my way home from school. He and his mates are always hanging round the swings. They smoke and they have spitting competitions. They go as high as they can on the swings and see who can spit the furthest. It's disgusting. A few of them were sitting on the roundabout going round slowly. He'd jumped off and stood in front of me. I'd been scared stiff. He'd put his face right close to mine.

'Who are you for, Churchill or Attlee?'

I hadn't known what he was on about.

'C'mon, who are you for, Churchill or Attlee?'

I hadn't known what to say. I wasn't for either of them. He'd put his face even closer, our noses were nearly touching.

'I'm only askin' you once more, kid. Churchill or Attlee, who are you for?'

'Churchill . . .'

He'd smiled.

'That's all right, then.'

And he'd gone back to the roundabout.

I dread to think what would have happened if I'd said Attlee. I'd only said Churchill 'cos he was the Prime Minister. Then, when I got home I found out he wasn't.

'Who's Attlee, Mum?'

'Lay a place for your Auntie Doreen, she's coming round to set my hair.'

I got another plate from the cupboard and a knife and fork out of the drawer.

'How many times do I have to tell you, fork on the left, knife on the right.'

'Sorry.'

She changed them all round, I'm always getting them wrong.

'This lad asked me who I was for, Churchill or Attlee? I didn't know what he was talking about. I've never heard of Attlee, who is he?'

She looked at me.

'You've never heard of Mr Attlee?'

I shook my head.

'Mr Clement Attlee, you've never heard of him?'

I shook my head again.

'No. Who is he?'

Now it was my mum's turn to shake her head.

'Well, I'll go to Sheffield! I don't know what they teach you at that school?'

'Who is he?'

I heard the key in the front door and then my Auntie Doreen coming down the hall.

'Sorry I'm late, stocktaking at work. Couldn't get away.'

My mum took one of the forks off the table and went over to the cooker.

'You're all right, Doreen, these potatoes need a couple more minutes. Hey, you'll never believe this. Ask his lordship here who the Prime Minister is.'

I knew that.

'He knows who the Prime Minister is, don't you, love?'

She bent down and gave me a kiss and ruffled my hair.

''Course I do. Mr Churchill.'

They looked at each other and my Auntie Doreen started laughing.

'No, love, Mr Attlee's Prime Minister, he has been for the last six years, since 1945.'

My mum wasn't laughing.

'It's not funny, Doreen. It makes you wonder what they're teaching them at school when they don't even know the name of the Prime Minister.'

I couldn't understand it. I'd always thought it was Mr Churchill. My mum was always going on about him, what a great Prime Minister he was.

'But, Mum, you're always saying what a good Prime Minister he was and how we wouldn't have got through the

53

war if it hadn't been for him. Him and that Tommy Handley off the wireless.'

She started laughing as well. She gave me a hug.

'He was – during the war. He was wonderful, wasn't he, Doreen?'

My Auntie Doreen was hanging her coat up and tutting to herself.

'Wonderful. Inspiring. And how did we show our appreciation after the war? After he'd saved us from that madman Hitler? We kicked him out and voted Attlee and his lot in. Disgusting.'

My mum took the pan of potatoes over to the kitchen sink and poured the water out.

'He's not done a bad job, Mr Attlee, he's a good peace-time leader.'

'I don't want to talk about it! Makes my blood boil!'

I'd never seen her so cross. She sat down at the table but she'd forgotten to take her hat off.

'You've still got your hat on, Auntie Doreen.'

She didn't say anything, just sat there tapping her middle finger on the table.

'Wait till next Thursday, we'll see who's Prime Minister then. And it won't be your precious Clement Attlee, you mark my words.'

I wondered what was happening next Thursday. My mum put the potatoes into a dish and brought them over to the table.

'He's not my "precious Clement Attlee". I'm just saying he's done a good job. I think he's honest and honourable.'

I didn't like my mum and my Auntie Doreen arguing like this.

'What's happening next Thursday, Auntie Doreen?'

She wasn't listening to me.

'Well, you voted for him, didn't you? You're just like our dad, Labour through and through.'

My mum slammed the saucepan down on the table.

'Who I vote for is my own private business. It's nothing to do with you.'

I didn't like this. I wished I'd never asked who Attlee was now.

'What's happening next Thursday, Mum?'

She wasn't listening either, she was still going on at my Auntie Doreen.

'And what was it our mother always used to say, Doreen? Never discuss politics or religion at the dinner table!'

They both went quiet and we ate our tea. Sausage, potato and mashed-up turnip. I mashed my potato up as well and mixed it in with the turnip and some margarine. It was lovely. But nobody was talking. I didn't like it.

'What's happening next Thursday?'

Neither of them said anything, they just carried on with their tea. Then my Auntie Doreen got up and put her arm round my mum.

'I'm sorry, Freda, you're right, I spoke out of turn and I apologise. I just get very emotional when we talk about Winston Churchill.'

My mum gave her a hug.

'I know. I'm sorry I snapped at you. Go on, sit down and enjoy your tea.'

And my mum gave her a kiss. I was glad. I didn't like them arguing. Mind you, I couldn't understand what it was all about. What does it matter who the Prime Minister is? What was 'labour through and through' and what did it have to do with my grandad? And what was happening next Thursday? I didn't say anything though. I just asked my mum for some more sausage, potatoes and turnip.

I found out what my Auntie Doreen had been talking about next morning when I got to school. Norbert and Keith Hopwood and a few of the others were in the playground talking to Albert, the school caretaker, and they let out this big cheer. I went over. Norbert was jumping up and down.

'We're gettin' the day off next Thursday, we don't have to come to school.'

'Why?'

'General election.'

'What's that?'

'Don't know, but we're gettin' the day off, that's all I'm bothered about.'

It turned out that the next Thursday was voting day and the general election is when people over twenty-one have to choose who should be the next Prime Minister. Albert told us all about it.

'So they'll be using our school as a polling station and

you lot'll be having the day off, you lucky tykes. You'll all be getting a letter to take home.'

My mum wasn't pleased when she saw it. The letter.

'Well, it's all right them saying there's no school next Thursday but what are we supposed to do, us working mothers? Leave you at home on your own all day?'

She put it on the kitchen table and folded her arms.

'What's it say?'

'It says there's no school next Thursday.'

She picked it up again and read it out loud.

'"Dear Parents,

"This is to inform you that next Thursday, 25th October, the school will be one of the nominated polling stations for the forthcoming general election. As a result the school will be closed to pupils and I am writing to ask you to make alternative arrangements for your children . . ."'

She screwed it up and threw it on the fire.

'That's nice, isn't it? "Alternative arrangements"? What am I supposed to do? Take a day off work to look after you?'

'It's all right, Mum, you don't have to look after me, some of us are gettin' together. It's all arranged.'

She looked at me.

'What's arranged?'

'We're going to play.'

'Where? Not in the street.'

'No, 'course not, we'll go to the park.'

57

She frowned at me.

'And what happens if it rains?'

It wouldn't bother us if it rained, we'd be all right.

'We'll be all right, we'll go into Arkwright Hall till it stops.'

Arkwright Hall's great. It's a museum and you can get in for free. A lot of it's boring, just pictures and statues and stuff. But there's one room with machines in that show you how the steam engine and electricity and the telephone work and you can go on them. We often go in there. We usually get thrown out though, specially when you go with Norbert, he's always messing about.

'Arkwright Hall? And what happens when you get thrown out?'

'We won't.'

'You usually do.'

'We don't. Anyway, Keith Hopwood says we can go to his house, his gran lives with them. And we thought we could go to the pictures in the afternoon, those who get the money. *Canyon Raiders* is on at the Essoldo. It's a U, we can go in on our own.'

'And what about your dinner? Have you thought about that?'

We had.

'Fish and chips from Pearson's.'

She didn't say anything. Just looked at me.

'Who's "we" anyway? Who's in this little gang who've decided what they're going to do on election day?'

I told her. Me, Tony, Keith Hopwood, David

Holdsworth, Alan McDougall maybe, if his mum let him. I didn't tell her that Norbert would be with us, she doesn't like him.

'Well, as long as it doesn't include that Norbert Lightowler, you always get into trouble when he's around.'

I shrugged my shoulders.

'Not sure what he's doin'.'

'W-w-what shall we d-d-do then?'

It must've been about the third or fourth time Keith had asked and every time one of us had said the same thing back: 'Don't know, what do you want to do?' This time it was David Holdsworth.

'Don't know, what do you want to do?'

We were sitting on the wall in Keith's back garden. Me, Keith, David Holdsworth and Norbert. Alan McDougall's mum hadn't let him come and Tony had gone with his big sister to his gran's in Wakefield. I couldn't see what was wrong with going to the park like we'd said we were going to, but none of the others wanted to, specially Norbert.

'Park's borin', we're always goin' t'park, let's do summat different.'

All the others agreed but nobody could think of anything – except Norbert.

'Hang on, I've got an idea . . .'

I'd told my mum we were going to the park.

'I've got a great idea . . .'

I'd told her that I didn't know what Norbert would be doing.

'What about this . . . ?'

She'd said I always get into trouble when he's around.

'Let's go and play on the bombsite!'

They all thought it was a great idea. No! I wanted to go to the park like I'd told my mum. Go to Arkwright Hall if it rained. Have fish 'n' chips from Pearson's. Go and see *Canyon Raiders* in the afternoon. That's what I'd told my mum we were going to do. All of us. I'd got the money in my pocket.

'No, I think we should go to the park. We can go into Arkwright Hall if it rains.'

Norbert said Arkwright Hall was boring as well.

'It's all statues and old paintings. Anyway, I'm banned from there, I broke that machine that shows you how electricity works. I wor only playin' on it.'

David Holdsworth said the bombsite was better than the park.

'Yeah, we'll play there till dinner-time then go to Pearson's for us fish and chips, then go and see *Canyon Raiders*. It starts at quarter past one.'

I didn't want to go to the bombsite, my mum'd go mad. She was always telling me to keep away from there.

'You've got a lovely park you can go and play in and what do you lot do? Go and hang around that horrible bombsite. Why do you have to play there?'

'It's fun.'

She didn't understand, the bombsite's great. It's where a doodlebug landed in the war, Miss Taylor had told us all about it at school. There's all these bombed-out houses, nobody lives there any more and we run in and out playing commandos.

'Fun? It's dangerous. I don't want you playing around that bombsite any more, will you promise me . . . ? Promise!'

If it hadn't been for Mr Churchill and Mr Attlee I wouldn't have broken my promise. We'd have been at school and I wouldn't have gone to the bombsite. And I wouldn't have gone into the air-raid shelter.

No, that's daft, it was my own fault. I shouldn't have listened to Norbert. I shouldn't have gone with the others.

'You d-d-don't have to c-c-come with us. We'll see you at P-Pearson's.'

I watched them all going off. I didn't want to be on my own. What was I going to do all morning?

'Hang on, I'm coming with you.'

Norbert was right, it *was* better than the park. We were playing World War Two and me and Keith were against Norbert and David, we were the English and they were the Germans. Norbert always wants to be the German side. They were in the upstairs of this bombed-out house shooting down at us. He was wearing this old gas mask he'd found. He's mad, Norbert, it was probably full of germs but he still put it on, he wasn't bothered.

'S'all right, it's a good gas mask this, might be worth some money, I'm goin' to show it to my dad.'

I threw a pretend hand grenade that would have killed them but they carried on shooting.

'Norbert, you're dead, I threw a hand grenade.'

He shouted something but you couldn't tell what he was saying 'cos of his gas mask.

'Y'what? I can't tell what you're saying.'

He pulled it off.

'My gas mask protected me.'

'A gas mask can't protect you against a hand grenade. Anyway it's your turn, we died last time, didn't we, Keith?'

'Yeah, w-we died last t-t-time.'

David put his hand up.

'Truce. We're comin' down.'

We stopped playing World War Two and sat on this old sofa. There were tons of sofas and beds and armchairs around. And old stoves and kiddies' cots. And wardrobes and cupboards and old baths. All sorts of stuff. I can't remember the war, I was only a baby. I'm glad a doodlebug didn't fall on our house.

David had a bar of Five Boys chocolate. He gave us a piece each and he had two. It was his chocolate so it was only fair. It was nice of him to give us any, I wouldn't have.

'My mum said I had to.'

It was still nice of him, he didn't have to do what his mum told him. My mum had told me not to play on the bombsite. She'd made me promise. But I was here, wasn't I?

'If I hadn't given you any she'd have found out, she'd have asked me. She can always tell when I'm lying.'

So can *my* mum. I wish I hadn't come.

'I'm bored here now, let's go somewhere else.'

They all agreed. I couldn't believe it. Mind you, we'd been there for more than an hour and we'd had enough of World War Two. David said he fancied going to the park for a bit before we went for us fish and chips.

'We can have a go on the boating lake if it's open.'

Norbert said he couldn't, he wouldn't be allowed on.

'I'm banned. Ever since I turned that canoe upside down. Hey, I'll wear my gas mask, he won't recognise me, come on!'

We set off across the bombsite. I was so glad, I wouldn't have to lie to my mum now, I could tell her that we'd been in the park, got fish and chips from Pearson's like we said we would and gone to see *Canyon Raiders*. I just wouldn't tell her we'd played on the bombsite. Yes, I felt much better. Everything was all right now.

And it would have been if we hadn't bumped into Arthur Boocock. He was hanging around by the entrance to the air-raid shelter.

'Where you lot off to?'

'Park.'

We all said it together. David told him we were going on the boating lake. I wanted him to shut up, I didn't want Boocock coming with us, I hate him.

'I thought you were banned, Lightowler, for capsizing that boat.'

'I didn't capsize it, I turned it over and it wor a canoe

63

not a boat and I'm goin' to wear this, he won't recognise me.'

Norbert put the gas mask on. Boocock snorted.

'You look stupid. Anyway, t'boating lake's closed, it's only open on Saturdays and Sundays this time of year.'

Trust Boocock to muck everything up, I bet none of them would go now. We had to go to the park so I wouldn't have to lie to my mum.

'Me and Gordon were down there earlier on. S'all closed up.'

Him and Gordon Barraclough. I hate them. Norbert took the gas mask off.

'Where is Barraclough?'

Norbert hates Barraclough as much as I do. More. They're always fighting.

'In there.'

He pointed towards the air-raid shelter. He couldn't mean in there. Nobody goes in there. It's horrible. It's where all the people ran to when the doodlebug came down.

'I've bet him that I can stay in there longer than he can.'

I'd peeped through the door once. It's pitch black, you can't see a thing.

'He's m-m-mad, I w-wouldn't go in there.'

Just then there was a scream, the door opened and Barraclough came running out. He looked scared stiff.

'There's someone in there, I heard something.'

We all gathered round him asking what he'd heard.

'I don't know, a noise, it were like a cough and I heard footsteps. I didn't like it.'

It was good seeing Barraclough scared like this. We were the ones usually scared of things, not him. Everybody laughed at him.

'You can't see a thing and I'm tellin' you, I heard summat, there wor a cough.'

Norbert started teasing him.

'Maybe there's a ghost in there, maybe that's what you heard, a ghost with a cough.'

He started waving his arms around and making ghost sounds and Barraclough went for him. Me and Keith had to pull them apart.

'I bet none of you lot'd go in there. Come on, I dare yer, any of yer!'

Arthur said he had a better idea.

'Look, there's six of us 'ere, we'll all put sixpence in and the one who stays in the longest keeps the money. C'mon, a tanner each, that'll be three shillings for the winner.'

Norbert put his hand in his pocket.

'Here y'are, Arthur. Come on, Barraclough, put your money in.'

Barraclough didn't look too keen but he couldn't back down in front of Boocock and Norbert and he handed over his sixpence. Boocock turned to me, Keith and David.

'What about you three?'

I looked at the others. I didn't want to waste my money, Boocock was bound to stay in the longest. Then David took his money out.

'Might as well. You never know, I might win.'

I looked at him. How could he think he could beat Boocock? None of us would beat him, he wins at everything.

Well, me and Keith weren't going to waste our money.

'Come on, Keith, we'll go to the park.'

But he had his hand in his pocket.

'Keith, you said Barraclough was mad goin' in the air-raid shelter, you said you'd never go in there.'

He got his sixpence out.

'Yeah, b-but this is for m-m-money. Here y'are, Arthur, here's my t-tanner.'

They were all looking at me now. What was I supposed to do, be the only one not to do the dare? I'd never live it down, specially with Keith doing it. He's softer than me. I held out my sixpence. Norbert took it, gave it to Boocock and asked him how were we going to time it.

'How are we goin' to know who stays in the longest?'

'As soon as the first person goes through the door, all of us outside'll count.'

'And who's goin' to go first?'

'We'll do "One potato, Two potato" to decide the order.'

We all got in a circle round Boocock.

'One potato, two potato, three potato, four, five potato, six potato, seven potato, more – you're first, Keith.'

Norbert was second, then Barraclough. David was after Barraclough, then Boocock and I was last. Boocock pushed Keith towards the door.

'W-why do I have to g-go f-first?'

''Cos you were first to go out in "One potato, Two", now go on.'

Keith looked at us all, went in and we shut the door behind him.

'1–2–3–4 . . .'

We only got as far as 9 before the door opened and he came running out.

'It's horrible in th-there, you c-c-can't see anything.'

Everybody laughed 'cos he'd only got as far as 9. I was hoping I'd last *that* long. Next it was Barraclough's go. He went to the door and turned back.

'Keith, did you hear anything?'

Boocock laughed.

'He didn't stay in there long enough!'

'W-wait till you lot g-go in, you w-w-won't be laughing then.'

'1–2–3–4 . . .'

We all counted out loud.

'10–11–12 . . .'

He was beating Keith.

'15–16–17 . . .'

I didn't want Barraclough to win.

'28–29–30 . . .'

He came running out.

'I heard it again. The cough. There's someone in there, I'm tellin' yer.'

David went in and came out again straight away.

'It's too dark, I don't like it.'

Norbert went in.

'1–2–3–4 . . .'

He was inside for ages, we counted up to 53. He looked white when he came out but he had this big smile on his face.

'Beat that, Boocock!'

Then he threw up. Arthur Boocock went in.

'1–2–3–4 . . .'

I didn't want him to win the money.

'19–20–21 . . .'

I just prayed he wasn't going to beat Norbert.

'41–42–43 . . .'

Oh no, he was going to win, wasn't he?

'49–50–51–52 . . .'

Blooming Boocock!

'53–54–55 . . .'

The door opened and he came running out, holding up his arms like he was the champion.

'Shall I take the money now?'

Norbert pointed at me.

'Get lost, he's got his go yet.'

Boocock laughed at me. He was right, he might as well have taken the money. There was no way I was going to stay in there as long as him. I probably wouldn't stay in as long as David or Keith. I went to the entrance. Boocock was still laughing.

'Go on, we're not goin' to start counting till you're inside.'

They closed the door. It went black.

'1 . . .'

I could hear them counting outside.

'2 . . .'

It was horrible. I couldn't see a thing.

'3 . . .'

Three? Why are they counting slower for me?

'4 . . .'

I've nearly stayed as long as David . . . nearly. At least I won't be the worst.

'5 . . .'

Only 5? I've been in here for ages, how can I only be on 5? I'm going. I'm getting out.

'6–7 . . .'

I'll stay long enough to beat Keith then I'm going, just another couple of seconds.

'8 . . .'

Nearly there. At least I've beaten Keith and David. Right, I'm off, Boocock can have the blooming money, I'm not staying here any longer.

'10–11 . . .'

I'm in double figures. How long did Barraclough stay? Thirty? No, I can't stay that long, that's twice as long again.

'13–14 . . .'

'14? That's nearly 15 – halfway to Barraclough's score.

Maybe . . . maybe . . . I closed my eyes. I don't know why, it made no difference in the dark.

'15 . . .'

No, I can't stay any longer, I'm off. I've had enough. I opened my eyes again – and that's when I saw it – the light shining in my face. There was a man standing there, shining a torch in my face.

'16 . . .'

I tried to scream but I couldn't. Nothing would come out. My heart was pounding inside my chest.

'17 . . .'

I tried to run. I couldn't move. I was paralysed. Help! Help! No sound came out. I wanted to shout help but no sound would come out. Help!

'18 . . .'

He started coming towards me. Help! Help! Why won't any sound come out? He was horrible, he had these scabs all over his face and he was all whiskery.

'19–20–21 . . .'

'Don't vorry, zere iss nossink to be frightened of.'

I *was* frightened. He spoke funny, in this foreign accent.

'22 . . .'

Suddenly he grabbed hold of me by the shoulders. I was terrified. He's going to kill me. Help! Nothing's coming out. Why did I break my promise? Why did I come to the bombsite? Help! Please don't kill me. Then he smiled.

'I can help you. You can beat ze bully boy. Stay here for a few more secondz and you vill vin your competition.'

'27–28–29 . . .'

'You see, you are almost half of za vay zere.'

He smiled again and started coughing.

'Excuse me, I haff a bad chest, it makes me cough.'

Barraclough had been right, he had heard someone cough.

70

'Please, don't tell ze uzzer boys zat I live here.'

I couldn't believe it. He lived in the air-raid shelter?

'Zat's vy I have zis cough, it's very damp in here.'

Why would he want to live in the air-raid shelter?

'32–33–34 . . .'

'Why do you live here? It's horrible.'

He smiled again. His eyes were watering a bit.

'My dear boy, I am lucky to haff zis. I came from Germany viz nuzzink.'

He held out his hand.

'My name is Rudi.'

I shook it and told him my name.

'Where do you sleep?'

He shone the torch over to another part of the air-raid shelter and started walking.

'49–50–51 . . .'

I followed him.

'52–53 . . .'

There was a walled-off bit, like a separate room, and he pointed his torch into the corner. There was a mattress on the ground, an old sofa, a chair and a small cupboard. He must have found them all on the bombsite. And there were lots of empty tin cans. The smell was horrible. How could he live here? It was disgusting. Where did he go to the lavatory?

'56–57–58 . . .'

'You are ze vinner. Go! But please, don't tell anybody zat I am here. Ziss is our secret. *Ja?*'

I nodded and he shone his torch so that I could see my

way to the door. When I turned back to say thank you, it was all black again, he'd gone.

'Thanks, Rudi!'

'62–63–64 . . .'

I opened the door and the daylight made me blink for a couple of seconds. I could hear Norbert, Keith and David cheering, then I saw Norbert jumping up and down.

'Go on, hand it over, Boocock, he's the winner.'

Boocock and Barraclough couldn't believe that I'd stayed in the longest. None of them could. *I* couldn't believe it.

I was sitting in the kitchen watching my mum unload the shopping.

'Well, did you have a nice day, love? Did you go to the park like you said you would?'

She had her back to me. She didn't see me blushing.

'Yes.'

I wasn't lying. We had gone to the park, me, Norbert, Keith and David, but only after I'd said I'd buy them an ice-cream out of my winnings.

'And we went to see *Canyon Raiders*, it was good. And we got fish and chips from Pearson's like we said we would.'

'So, you had a good day, then?'

'Yeah.'

I wanted to tell her about Rudi, the German man, living in the air-raid shelter. How he lived there in the dark, sleeping on an old mattress, eating stuff out of tins. But I couldn't, could I? I'd have to tell her that I'd been down to the bombsite. That I'd broken my promise. *Twice.*

I'd gone back to the air-raid shelter after the pictures.

'Rudi? . . . Rudi? I've brought you something to eat . . . I thought you might be hungry . . . Hello . . . Rudi?'

I saw the light from his torch and then I heard him coming towards me. He called out my name.

'I've brought you some fish and chips, Rudi.'

I'd bought them from Pearson's out of my winnings. I didn't want the money anyway, I felt guilty.

He couldn't believe it. He took hold of them.

'Zey are varm. Sank you, sank you. You are a goot boy.'

His eyes filled with tears, I felt sorry for him. He was quite small, not much bigger than me, and he looked so old.

'I've got to go, Rudi. Sorry. My mum'll be home soon.'

He came over and gave me a hug. He smelt horrible. It made me feel sick. I pushed him away.

'You're squashing your fish and chips.'

My mum was putting her coat back on.

'Now listen, love, me and your Auntie Doreen have got to go and vote, I'm just popping round to fetch her. We won't be long.'

She picked up her handbag and went towards the back door.

'Mum – I've got something to tell you.'

'Oh, yes?'

She turned round.

'What, love?'

I looked at her.

'Norbert Lightowler came with us today, but we didn't get into any trouble.'

She smiled and came over.

'You've told me now, that's all that matters. As long as you tell me the truth.'

She gave me a kiss.

'You're a good lad.'

I felt sick.

'Rudi . . . Are you there . . . ? It's me . . .'

After school on the Friday I spent my last sixpence on a Cornish pastie and took it to the air-raid shelter for him.

'I've got you some food.'

He came shuffling round the corner shining his torch.

'Oh, you are a kind boy, haff you brought me fish and chips again? Zey vere most delicious.'

'No, sorry. I only had sixpence left. I've got you a Cornish pastie.'

I held out the paper bag.

'It's cold though. Sorry.'

'You are a goot boy.'

'Will you be all right?'

He smiled and ruffled my hair.

'Don't vorry, I vill manage. I am a survivor. Now go home or your muzzer vill vorry about you.'

*

74

'This is the BBC Home Service. Here is the six o'clock news and this is Alvar Liddell reading it. Mr Winston Churchill is back in 10 Downing Street. At seventy-seven he is tonight forming his first peacetime government after the Conservative Party's narrow general-election victory. Mr Churchill says he savours the challenge of a new beginning . . .'

'Is that good, Mum? Mr Churchill winning?'

She nodded at my Auntie Doreen who was reading the evening paper.

'Your Auntie Doreen obviously thinks so. Look at her. It's all right you smiling, Doreen, he only just got in.'

My Auntie Doreen put her paper down.

'Winnie's back, that's what matters. The country has spoken.'

My mum got up.

'Yes, well, Alvar Liddell's spoken. You've had your moment of glory.'

She went over to the wireless and switched it off. My Auntie Doreen went back to her paper.

'Actually, Freda, there's a very interesting article here. It's about Rudolf Hess. You know he made that secret flight to Britain? Well, according to this, he lived here for a while, in this road.'

My mum didn't say anything for a minute, just looked at her.

'Rudolf Hess lived in this road? Rubbish!'

My Auntie Doreen held out the paper.

'Well, according to this . . .'

My mum took it and started reading. I wondered what they were talking about.

'Who's Rudolf Hess?'

They weren't listening. My mum was still reading the paper.

'I don't like to think of that Rudolf Hess living round here, makes my stomach turn.'

'Who is he? Who's Rudolf Hess?'

My mum gave the paper back to my Auntie Doreen.

'Don't they teach you anything at that school? He was a German. A Nazi. He was Adolf Hitler's deputy. He came here during the war, secretly.'

She picked up the paper again.

'I can't believe he came here. They said he landed in Scotland. Why would he come here?'

No! Oh no! That's why he's hiding in the air-raid shelter. That's who he is! My stomach churned. He's a Nazi. Rudi's a Nazi. He's Adolf Hitler's deputy. He's Rudolph Hess and I've been giving him fish and chips and Cornish pasties. No! I'm a traitor. I'm a traitor!

'What's the matter, love, what's wrong?'

I couldn't stop crying and I was shaking. I couldn't stop myself from shaking.

'It was Mr Churchill's fault. Him and that Mr Attlee. If it hadn't been for them none of it would have happened. We wouldn't have had the day off. I'd have been at school.'

'What's wrong with him, Doreen?'

'I'm a traitor, Mum, I'm a traitor. I know where Rudolf

Hess is. I've been giving him fish and chips and Cornish pasties.'

My mum held me tight.

'You'd better fetch the doctor, Doreen, I think he's having a fit. He's talking gibberish.'

My Auntie Doreen started to go but I got hold of her arm.

'No, Mum. I broke my promise, I'm sorry. I went down to the bombsite. I know where Rudolf Hess is. He's living in the air-raid shelter. I'm sorry, Mum, I'm sorry.'

The tears were rolling down my face. I couldn't stop crying.

'I'm a traitor, I'm a traitor.'

'I don't know who you've been talking to, love, but it's not Rudolf Hess. He's in prison in Germany. They sent him back in 1945.'

Me mum got hold of me.

'Now you've told me you been down on the bombsite, I won't be cross with you, I just want you to tell me what happened. Who have you been talking to?'

They were looking at me, my mum and my Auntie Doreen, and my mum was wiping my face with a damp towel.

'You promise you won't be cross?'

'I promise, I give you my word. Now, just start at the beginning. Tell me what happened.'

And I did. I told her everything.

My mum was right, he wasn't Rudolf Hess. She told the police all about it and they went round to the air-raid shelter. They took him away and found him somewhere nicer to live. It turned out he *was* from Germany but he'd escaped *from* the Nazis. His name was Rudi Klein and he'd lost all his family in the war. They'd been killed by Hitler in a camp or something. I didn't understand and my mum said she'd explain it to me when I got older.

She broke her promise though. She did get cross with me.

'Just think if you'd gone into that air-raid shelter and it hadn't been that nice old man in there. If it had been . . . somebody . . . somebody . . .'

She was trying to think of the right word.

'The real Rudolf Hess?'

She looked at me.

'No, love, what I'm trying to tell you is that there are some really evil, wicked people in this world and it could have been someone . . . someone . . .'

Tears started coming into her eyes. She took hold of me by the shoulders. She held me really tight. It made me think of when Rudi got hold of me like that.

'You mean I could have been killed?'

That's when she started crying. She put her arms round me. I thought she was never going to let go.

THE BACK BEDROOM

I'd just got back from school and was hanging up my coat when my mum came down the stairs.

'Your Auntie Doreen's coming round in a minute, we're popping in to see Mrs Bastow.'

'Ooh, can I go with you?'

My mum goes to do her hair for her sometimes 'cos it's hard for Mrs Bastow to get out with her gammy leg. She gets paid for it but my mum doesn't like taking her money. I've heard her telling my Auntie Doreen.

'I don't like to, Doreen. I mean they're both pensioners. I'd rather she kept her money but she won't hear of it.'

'She'd pay a lot more if she went to the hairdresser's, and you're helping her out. She's not embarrassed to ask you if she's giving you money.'

'Mm, I suppose so . . .'

I'm glad my mum helps her out. I love going there with her. Mrs Bastow brings out the biscuit barrel and tells me to help myself and Mr Bastow lets me play on his model railway. He's always in charge but he lets me control the speed of the trains and switch switches and things. It's in the back bedroom upstairs and it takes up the whole room. You can hardly open the door. You have to squeeze in and crawl under this table and you stand in a space in the middle and watch all these model trains zooming round the tracks. It's great. Mr Bastow says it's his pride and joy. His sanctuary he calls it. I'm not sure Mrs Bastow likes it.

'He's obsessed, he's like a big kid with that railway. If he goes before me, God knows what I'm going to do with it. Takes up the whole back bedroom, y'know.'

I'd asked my mum what *would* happen to the model railway if Mr Bastow went before Mrs Bastow.

'Oh, I don't know, she doesn't mean it. Anyway, nobody's going anywhere.'

That was only a couple of weeks back.

'Ooh, can I go with you? Mr Bastow might let me play on the trains.'

We heard my Auntie Doreen letting herself in. She called down the hall.

'Sorry to take so long, Freda, I didn't want to go round there in my work clothes. I went home to change first.'

She came into the kitchen and that's when it dawned on me. My mum had changed out of her work clothes as well.

'I'm not going round there to do her hair, love. We're going to pay our respects. Mr Bastow passed away this morning.'

'Passed away?'

My Auntie Doreen took hold of my hands.

'He's died, love, this morning.'

80

I'd thought that's what she'd meant.

'Mrs Bastow found him in the front room in his favourite chair.'

'Dead?'

'I'm afraid so. That's why your mum and I are going round. To pay our respects.'

I wondered what was going to happen to the model railway.

'How is she, Freda? Have you heard?'

My mum shrugged and told her that from what Mrs Priestley was saying, when she saw her in the butcher's, Mrs Bastow was bearing up. I was still thinking about the railway.

'I'll come with you, Mum.'

She looked at me.

'I'd like to pay my respects as well.'

My Auntie Doreen smiled and put her arm round me.

'I think that'd be lovely, Freda. She'd really appreciate it. You liked Mr Bastow, didn't you, love?'

'Yeah . . .'

My mum didn't say anything, just carried on looking. I knew what she was thinking and she was right.

'Yes, and he liked playing on his model railway. Don't you think you're going to be playing on that railway today, young man.'

''Course not. I just want to pay my respects, don't I?'

'Do you?'

'Yeah.'

My Auntie Doreen said she thought she was being a bit hard on me. She wasn't.

On the way we stopped off to get some flowers for Mrs Bastow. We went to Middleton's in Cranley Road but my mum didn't like the look of them.

'They'll not last more than a day or two, they won't.'

My Auntie Doreen agreed.

'And they're expensive. There's that florist the other end of St Barnabas Street. It's a bit out of the way but I think they're very reasonable and good quality.'

In one of the houses in St Barnabas Street we passed an old man sitting in a wheelchair, staring out of the front-room window into the street. I wouldn't have even noticed him if my mum hadn't stopped to talk. Well, she didn't talk exactly, she mouthed at him through the window. 'How are you, Mr Shackleton . . . ? All right . . . ? Lovely . . .' The old man didn't seem to see her, he just carried on staring as if we weren't there. There was a bit of spit dribbling out of his mouth. My mum waved and mouthed again, 'Bye-bye then, Mr Shackleton' and then said 'Shame' to my Auntie Doreen as they carried on walking. I looked at the old man. The bit of spit was down to his chin and his eyes were watering, but they never blinked. He was just staring straight ahead like he couldn't see me. I felt sorry for him. I gave him my own little wave and I was just about to go when I saw his hand move. I wasn't sure, it was so slow, but . . . yes, it was definitely moving.

'C'mon, love, the florist'll be closing soon!'

'Comin', Mum!'

I looked back and his hand was up a bit higher. He looked like he was trying to wave back. He moved his fingers. Just a bit. He *was*, he was waving back. I waved again, moving my fingers slowly like he was doing. He still didn't blink. He stared like he couldn't see me, like he was looking through me, and the dribble of spit was hanging from his chin now. Then his mouth moved. He was smiling at me, I'm sure he was. My mum was shouting for me to hurry up. I waved again and ran down the street and caught up with them.

'Who's that old man, Mum?'

'Eric Shackleton and I don't think he's that old. What is he, Doreen, forty-five? Fifty?'

My Auntie Doreen reckoned he was about fifty. That seemed old to me. She told me that he used to be a roofer, he mended roofs and about four or five years back he'd fallen off this house.

'He broke his back. He's been in a wheelchair ever since. He was a lovely man, wasn't he, Freda? Do anything for anybody he would.'

'Yes, and so handsome. Must've been over six foot tall. Breaks my heart to see him like that, sitting there, staring out that window. That's all he does all day.'

They both said 'Shame' again and we went into the florist's.

They took ages deciding which flowers to get for Mrs Bastow. The lady in the shop pointed to some blue ones.

'Irises are always acceptable whatever the occasion.'

My mum wasn't sure.

'It's not an occasion, I'm afraid, it's a bereavement. The lady lost her husband this morning.'

'You can't go wrong with irises, love.'

While the flower lady wrapped them up my mum chose a card that said 'With Sympathy' and wrote on the back.

'What are you puttin', Mum?'

She showed me. It said, 'Sorry for your sad loss, with love from Freda and Doreen'.

'Go on, you write something.'

'What shall I put?'

'It's up to you, you're big enough.'

I wrote, 'I'll miss you, Mr Bastow', signed my name and showed it to my mum.

'Aw . . . Look at that, Doreen.'

What I really meant was, I'll miss playing on the model railway with you, Mr Bastow.

'Aw, that's lovely. Very nice.'

'Thanks, Auntie Doreen . . .'

It was when we turned into her street that I said it.

'She must be worried about the model railway, y'know.'

They looked at me.

'He's gone before her, hasn't he?'

'What on earth are you talking about?'

That's the trouble with my mum, she never remembers anything anybody says.

'That's what Mrs Bastow said. If he goes before me, what am I going to do with it? Don't you remember?'

84

I thought she was going to clout me.

'For goodness sake, she's just lost her husband. The last thing she'll be thinking about will be model railways!'

'It takes up the whole back bedroom . . .'

She just caught my ear. Didn't hurt.

When we got to the house the curtains were closed. My Auntie Doreen said that's what you do when someone dies.

'Even when it's light outside?'

'It's custom, love, when someone dies, you draw the curtains. It's a mark of respect.'

'Oh . . .'

We were sitting round the kitchen table drinking tea. Mrs Bastow was sniffing into her hanky. She was holding a photo of Mr Bastow. I was wondering if I could take another fig roll from the biscuit barrel. She'd told me to help myself but I'd already had two. No, I'd better not.

'I can't believe it. I can't believe he's gone.'

She wiped her eyes.

'He was just beginning to enjoy his retirement.'

My mum held out the box of tissues for her and squeezed her hand.

'I know.'

'I can't believe it. I just can't believe it. Have another biscuit, love.'

I looked at my mum. Mrs Bastow pushed the biscuit barrel to my side of the table.

'Never mind looking at her, you help yourself, they're there to be eaten.'

My mum gave me a nod and I took another fig roll, then changed my mind and took a digestive instead.

'Don't touch them and then put them back!'

Mrs Bastow wasn't bothered.

'Take as many as you like, love, I'll not want them, I've got no appetite.'

My Auntie Doreen told her she had to eat.

'You've got to keep your strength up, Mrs Bastow.'

'I know, I know . . .'

She nodded and sighed. My mum and my Auntie Doreen sighed and it all went quiet. I finished the biscuit and went to get another, but my mum stopped me with one of her looks.

'She said I could!'

'Who's "she"?'

'Mrs Bastow. She said I could.'

Mrs Bastow nodded.

'He's all right. And that was lovely what you wrote on that card, love, I really appreciate it. And those flowers. Lovely. Thank you.'

And she started crying again. My mum put her arm round her.

'When's the funeral, Mrs Bastow?'

I tried to eat the biscuit as quietly as I could. It was a garibaldi. It were lovely.

'I'm not sure. The undertaker's sorting it all out. Do you want to have a look at him?'

I nearly choked on the garibaldi. What did she mean, 'Have a look at him'? I thought he was dead.

'He's in the front room. He looks ever so peaceful in death.'

That's where she'd found him, in the front room, sitting in his favourite chair. And he's still there? And she wants us to have a look at him? Why's he in the house when he's dead? I thought they got taken away. My mum stood up.

'That'd be very nice, Mrs Bastow, we'd like to pay our respects.'

I thought we'd come to pay our respects to *Mrs* Bastow, I didn't know you had to go and look at a dead body to pay your respects, I wouldn't have come. Then my Auntie Doreen stood up. So I did. Oh, I didn't fancy this at all. I didn't want to look at him dead in his favourite chair. My mum put her hand on my shoulder.

'You wait here, love, we won't be long.'

Oh, thanks, Mum, thanks. I don't have to go and pay my respects. Thanks. While they were in the front room looking at Mr Bastow I finished the garibaldi and then had another fig roll.

''Course he wasn't sitting in the chair, he was in a coffin! Wait till I tell your Auntie Doreen. Oh, I shouldn't laugh.'

We were back at home having our tea. I could hardly eat mine, I'd filled myself up on Mrs Bastow's biscuits. But I didn't let my mum see. I forced it down.

'Well, I didn't know, did I? She just said, did we want to have a look at him in the front room. I thought that was why she'd closed the curtains.'

She started clearing the table.

'That's nothing to do with it. Your Auntie Doreen told you, you always draw the curtains when somebody dies. Even if the coffin's upstairs. It's a custom, it lets people know there's been a bereavement. Come on, you're never going to finish, you've eaten that many biscuits. Anyway, that was a nice thing you did, offering to help Mrs Bastow like that.'

I put the lid back on the biscuit barrel. I'd better not have any more or I wouldn't be able to eat my tea . . . They seemed to have been in there a long time. I thought about Mr Bastow sitting in there. In his favourite chair. Dead . . . This was boring, waiting here when I could have been up in the back bedroom playing on the model railway. I bet Mr Bastow wouldn't have minded. I knew how to do it, all the switches and stuff. I bet he'd have been pleased. He was dead anyway, what did it matter? It was such a waste it not being used . . . I heard them coming down the hall. My mum sat Mrs Bastow down at the kitchen table.

'What you need, dear, is a nice cup of tea. Put the kettle on, Doreen.'

Oh no, not more tea. I wish I'd never come. So boring.

'I'm going to have to sort all his stuff out, y'know. I don't know where I'm going to start.'

What 'stuff' is she going to have to sort out?

'There's no hurry. You just get this funeral out of the way, then you can start thinking about things like that.'

Maybe she meant the railway. What was she going to do with it?

'I'll help you, Mrs Bastow.'

She came over and gave me a hug. She held on for ages. Her cardigan smelt funny. Sort of cabbage smell.

'He's special, this lad of yours. He does you credit.'

I set off for Mrs Bastow's. It was the Saturday after the funeral and I was going to help her sort the stuff out like I'd promised.

'And if she offers you any money you're not to take it, right?'

''Course not, Mum.'

I hadn't even thought about that, I was just hoping she might let me have a go on the railway.

'Come on in, love. This is ever so kind of you to give up your Saturday afternoon like this. You are a good lad. Now, what I want to do is make a start on that shed. You won't believe the stuff in there. He was a right hoarder was Mr Bastow, God bless him.'

I followed her into the hall, through the kitchen, out to the backyard.

'I've filled up the biscuit barrel. You've got a sweet tooth, haven't you? Nearly ate me out of house and home last time you were here, didn't you?'

She was laughing, I don't think she minded that I'd eaten so many biscuits. Anyway, she'd told me to help myself, hadn't she?

'Now, where did he keep that key?'

There was a big padlock on the shed door.

'I know, back in a minute. Do you want a glass of squash?'

She didn't ask if I wanted a biscuit.

'Please.'

While I was waiting I looked in through the window. There was lots of stuff. Tins of paint, a lawnmower and a rake and shovel and things. And all these magazines. But they were all on shelves in neat piles. Mrs Bastow came back with the key and some orange squash.

'It all looks quite tidy in there, Mrs Bastow.'

She took the padlock off and opened the door.

'Oh, it's tidy enough. He was always a tidy man was Mr Bastow, but there's a lot of junk in there. See all those paint pots? There'll only be a dribble in most of them, you mark my words. He couldn't throw anything away. And them magazines, they can all go.'

There were tons of them.

'What are they?'

'Oh, train magazines mostly.'

'He liked trains, didn't he.'

She sort of smiled.

'Oh, he was train mad, love. Used to drive me up the wall sometimes.'

She went quiet and shook her head. I was thinking that this'd be a good time to ask her. I was sure she wouldn't mind.

'Mrs Bastow . . . ?'

'Mm?'

'When I've finished, can I go and have a look at the model railway?'

I didn't ask her if I could play on it. I reckoned that if she let me have a look at it she'd be sure to say do you want to have a go. I mean, it wasn't as if I didn't know how it all worked.

'Y'what, love?'

'Can I go and have a look at the model railway when I've finished all the clearing out?'

She didn't say anything for a couple of seconds, just looked at me as if she didn't know what I was talking about.

'It's gone, love. It's not there . . .'

Now it was me looking at her. What was she talking about, gone?

'Mr Bastow got rid of it. About a week before he died.'

Got rid of it? Why would he get rid of it? He loved that railway.

'It took up the whole of that back bedroom, you couldn't clean in there. Mind you, when you look at what's happened it's a good job he did get rid of it, bless him. How would I have managed on my own?'

I couldn't believe it. He loved that model railway. Why would he get rid of it? You didn't have to clean in there. There was nothing to clean. It was all railway, wasn't it? There was no need to clean in there! I couldn't understand it.

'Shall we get started, love? Throw everything into these rubbish bags. I've got somebody coming round later to take 'em away. Only keep the paint pots that are heavy – there won't be more than a couple – otherwise get rid. Oh, and if you want to keep any of those train magazines for yourself, take as many as you like. I'll be glad to see the back of them.'

She went back into the house humming to herself. I started throwing the magazines into the rubbish bags. I didn't keep any for myself. I didn't want them. They were Mr Bastow's.

THE WHITE ROSE

Part One

A hundred and seventeen. A hundred and eighteen. I wish I'd never offered to clear out the shed for Mrs Bastow. A hundred and nineteen. I'd only done it 'cos I was hoping I might get a go on the model railway. A hundred and twenty, the last one! A hundred and twenty train magazines. I don't know why I counted them, I just did. And now they were all in the rubbish bags. Gone. Like the model railway. Mrs Bastow was surprised that I didn't keep any for myself. She didn't want them, so why should I? She didn't even care about the model railway. If Mr Bastow had said to me, 'Take as many as you like,' I would have. I'd have taken as many as I could have carried. But now I knew that before he'd died he'd got rid of the model railway – I don't know, I just thought, well, that's what Mr Bastow would have wanted me to do. Get rid of the magazines as well.

I went back into the shed and started clearing out all the old tins of paint. She was right, most of them were empty, there was hardly anything in any of them. One tin was heavier than the rest; it felt full so I put it on one side with the lawnmower and tools and other things that were going back in the shed. It looked like it had never been opened.

'Are you sure it's worth keeping, love? I don't want it if it's empty.'

She was coming down the garden with more rubbish bags.

'It's full, Mrs Bastow, I don't think it's even been opened.'

'Oh.'

I handed her the tin of paint. She screwed up her eyes.

'I can't read without my glasses. Does it say the colour? Read it out to me, love.'

'"Parkinson's Quality Paint".'

'No, the colour, love. I know it's Parkinson's, Mr Bastow always got his paint from there, they used to give him a good discount. What colour is it?'

'Er . . .'

I looked.

'Er . . . "Emulsion".'

'No, that's not the colour. What does it say on the label?'

I couldn't see a label.

'Er . . .'

Oh yes I could.

'"Lilac Heaven".'

She took it off me.

'Oh, I like lilac. That'll look good in the back bedroom.'

The model railway looked good in the back bedroom. Why did she make Mr Bastow get rid of it? That's what I wanted to say. But I didn't. I carried on clearing out the shed and she went back into the house with the tin of paint. It took me ages. I filled six bags with rubbish, empty paint tins mostly and a lot of old newspapers and broken plant pots. Then I started putting things back, the lawnmower and tools, a watering can and other stuff.

'Hang on, love, I just want you to give it a sweep. You can use that broom there.'

She came up the garden.

'You don't mind, do you, love?'

'No, 'course not, Mrs Bastow.'

'Course I minded. I wanted to go home, I'd had enough. It wasn't as if I was going to get a look at the railway now, never mind have a go on it.

'What about that cupboard? Did you clear it out?'

Opposite the shelves that the train magazines had been stacked on, there was a rickety old wooden cupboard with double doors. I hadn't even looked in it. I didn't know I was supposed to.

'No, Mrs Bastow, I didn't know I was—'

'It'll want clearing out, love, I'll bet you a pound to a penny.'

She opened the doors and it was full of rusty tins and smaller paint pots and old jam jars, some with paintbrushes in.

'This lot can go, it's all rubbish. Look, most of these brushes are brick hard, they're not worth keeping. Chuck the lot, then give the shed a good sweeping, there's a good lad. I'll go and get the dustpan and brush.'

I got another rubbish bag and started chucking

everything in. I just wanted to get home now. She hadn't even given me a biscuit. I didn't like Mrs Bastow any more.

I thought some of the stuff was worth keeping, jars full of screws and rubber bands. But she'd told me to get rid of it all, so I did. There was another pile of magazines. I thought they were more train magazines and I was just about to throw them into the rubbish when I saw the one on the top was called *The Wrestler*. It had a photo of this wrestler on the front. He was holding this big belt up in the air and it said:

The White Rose
Yorkshire's Own Champion

That's when I saw it.

Exclusive Interview with Eric Shackleton

Eric Shackleton? Eric Shackleton! That was the old man my mum and my Auntie Doreen had stopped to say hello to the day we went to pay our respects to Mrs Bastow. The day Mr Bastow had died. The old man in the wheelchair, sitting in his front room, staring out of the window. I'm sure my mum had said his name was Eric Shackleton. But she'd said he was a roof mender. I opened the magazine and inside there were more pictures spread across two pages. In one photo he had his arm round this other wrestler's head, he looked like he was yanking it off. In another he had him pinned on the floor. The biggest photo showed him holding his arms up in the air, with a big grin on his face, wearing the big belt. Underneath it said:

The White Rose Wins Fight of the Century
Shackleton Is New Yorkshire Champion

I looked at the photograph. Maybe this was another Eric Shackleton. It must be. Maybe she'd said *Eddie* Shackleton. Yeah, that was it, she'd said Eddie Shackleton not Eric Shackleton. I mean, why would my mum say he mended roofs when he was a champion wrestler? Anyway, I still asked Mrs Bastow if I could keep the magazines.

'Well, you do surprise me, young man, I'd have thought it'd be the train magazines you'd want, not these. Do you like wrestling then?'

'Yeah –' I didn't tell her why I wanted them in case it wasn't the man in the wheelchair. 'I love it.'

'Oh.'

She asked me if I wanted a carrier bag to take them home in.

'Yes, please, Mrs Bastow.'

I didn't go straight home, I went through the park and stopped off in the playground. It was deserted. I sat on one of the swings and got the magazines out of the carrier bag. *The Wrestler* was the only one with anything about Eric Shackleton in it, the others were old gardening magazines and there was one *Woman's Weekly*. I put *The Wrestler* back in the carrier bag and threw the rest into the bin. I still didn't go home, I wanted to see if 'The White Rose' was the man in the wheelchair, so I went round to St Barnabas Street.

I didn't know what number house it was, all I remembered was that it was about halfway up on the right. It turned out to be forty-seven and there he was in his wheelchair staring out of the window. I smiled and gave him a little wave. He didn't seem to see me, he was just staring ahead like before. I opened the carrier bag, peeped inside at the photograph on the front of *The Wrestler* and looked back at him. He was lifting his hand and waving at me like last time, moving his fingers really slowly. And I'm sure he was smiling. It could be him. He could be 'The White Rose'. I hoped it was.

'Mum, you know that man in the wheelchair that you said hello to the other day?'

She was getting our tea ready, cauliflower cheese. I don't know why we're always having cauliflower cheese, my mum knows I don't like it.

'Y'what, love?'

'That man in the wheelchair you said hello to the other day, what was his name?'

'What man's that? Be a love and get the knives and forks out.'

I started setting the table.

'That man in the wheelchair in St Barnabas Street, Mr Shackleton. You said hello to him when we went to pay our respects to Mrs Bastow. What was his first name?'

She told me. Eric. Eric Shackleton. I wondered if he really was 'The White Rose'.

'Why on earth do you want to know?'

I got *The Wrestler* out of the carrier bag and showed it to her. She looked at it for a minute. I waited for her to say something. It wasn't him, was it? 'Course it wasn't.

'Where did you get this?'

I told her I'd found it in Mrs Bastow's shed.

'You didn't just take it, did you? I hope you asked her.'

''Course I did. She was throwin' it out anyway. We threw out tons of stuff. Is that him, Mum, is that the same Eric Shackleton?'

It wasn't going to be him, I knew it. How could it be? An old man in a wheelchair like that, how could he be a champion wrestler?

'Do you know, I'd forgotten he was a wrestler.'

It *was* him. He was 'The White Rose' and he lived two streets away. How could she forget?

'He wasn't just a wrestler, Mum, he was the Yorkshire champion. He was 'The White Rose'. Yorkshire's own champion. Look!'

I pointed at the front of the magazine.

'You said he was a roofer. You said he mended roofs. How could you forget?'

She explained to me that he was a wrestler in his spare time, mending roofs was what he did for a living.

'He was semi-professional, love, he got paid a bit but not enough to live on.'

'But he was the champion, wasn't he? "The White Rose". It says so, look!'

I pointed at the photo of him holding up the belt. She didn't say anything for ages.

'He was. That was the name he used to fight under, "The White Rose". Do you know, I'd quite forgotten.'

She carried on staring at his picture.

'"The White Rose". 'Course he was. It must have been not long after that that he fell off that roof and broke his back. Yes, look.'

She read out the date on the top.

'October 1947. There you are, just before Christmas 1947, I remember now. The snow was terrible and he slipped. It was all in the papers.'

And then it happened. I'd been hoping like anything that the Mr Shackleton in St Barnabas Street would be the Eric Shackleton on the front of the magazine. And now my mum had told me it was, I wished it wasn't. I didn't want 'The White Rose' to be an old man in a wheelchair. I wanted him to be like he was in the photograph.

'He must've been a good wrestler, Mum.'

She nodded and held out the magazine for me to take back.

'He was . . . he was a good roofer too.'

I took *The Wrestler* and ran up to my bedroom.

'Don't be hanging round up there, your tea'll be ready in a minute and wash your hands!'

I wasn't bothered about him being a good roofer. I was wishing he'd never been a roofer. If he hadn't been a roofer he might still be the champion. I sat on my bed and looked at his picture and I started to cry.

On the Sunday we were getting ready to go to church, my mum, my Auntie Doreen and me. While we were in the hall getting our coats on my mum told her about the magazine I'd got from Mrs Bastow. My Auntie Doreen remembered him.

'Yes, he did a bit of wrestling, I think he was quite good.'

Did a bit of wrestling? Quite good? Didn't she remember he was the Yorkshire champion? I didn't say anything, I didn't want to talk about it.

'He wrestled under another name, what was it now? White Fang, White Flash. I know it was something funny.'

'He was "The White Rose", Auntie Doreen, what's funny about that? He was the Yorkshire champion!'

I didn't mean to shout, it just came out. I wanted them to stop talking about him like that. My mum turned on me.

'Who do you think you're talking to?'

'Sorry . . .'

'How dare you shout at your Auntie Doreen like that?'

'He's all right, Freda—'

'No he's not!'

And she made me take my windcheater off.

'I won't have you talking to your Auntie Doreen like that. You'll stay here till we get back.'

'He's all right, Freda.'

'I'll not have him shouting at you like that. Come on, Doreen.'

'Sorry, Auntie Doreen—'

SLAM! They'd gone.

I could hear my Auntie Doreen telling my mum that I wasn't a bad lad, that I didn't mean anything by it, but I knew my mum wouldn't come back for me. Not when she's in a mood like that.

I wasn't bothered. Church is boring anyway. And I hadn't meant to shout at her. I was just fed up with nobody remembering who he really was. I couldn't understand it. You'd have thought that day we saw him, the day we went to pay our respects to Mrs Bastow, you'd have thought my mum would have said, 'You see that man there, he was the Yorkshire wrestling champion. "The White Rose" they called him, he was famous.' No, all she remembered was that he was a roofer. And my Auntie Doreen, she wasn't much better. 'Did a bit of wrestling.' He was only the champion of bloody Yorkshire! And what did she call him? White Fang. What the bloody hell is White Fang? He was 'The White Rose'.

'The White bloody Rose – that was his bloody name!'

I kicked the front door and ran up to my bedroom. I knew it was wrong to swear, even to myself, specially on a Sunday, but I couldn't help it. I wished now I'd never found the blooming magazine. If I hadn't found it he'd have just been an old man in a wheelchair, wouldn't he? I don't suppose I'd have thought about him again. But now I knew he was 'The White Rose' I couldn't stop thinking about him.

I sat on my bed holding *The Wrestler*. I felt like tearing the thing up. Tearing it up and throwing it the dustbin.

'I'm sorry I shouted, Auntie Doreen.'

'I know you are, love, you didn't mean it.'

I looked at my mum.

'I didn't mean it, Mum.'

'I know, let's forget about it. Eat your dinner.'

We were having our Sunday roast. Pork with lots of crackling and crunchy potatoes. It were lovely. I felt better now.

'Can I have some more gravy, Mum?'

Yeah, much better.

'Over my potatoes, please, Mum.'

'Yes sir, three bags full sir.'

We were laughing now. It was all forgotten.

'When you've finished your dinner, go and get that magazine. I want your Auntie Doreen to see how handsome Eric Shackleton was before he had his accident.'

I sat on my bed holding *The Wrestler*. I felt like tearing the thing up. Tearing it up and throwing it in the dustbin. So I did. I went downstairs, out into the backyard and threw it away. But I didn't tear it up. As I was looking at it in the bin, staring at the picture of 'The White Rose' holding up his belt, I thought of poor Mr Shackleton sitting in his wheelchair staring out of his front window and I was glad I hadn't torn it up.

I could hear the church bells ringing as I ran down St

Barnabas Street. I got to his house and there he was sitting in his wheelchair staring out of the window. I smiled and gave my little wave. This time he smiled back quicker, I think he recognised me. I went closer and held up *The Wrestler* magazine and pointed to his picture. He looked at it for ages, smiled again and slowly lifted up his hand. Then I realised it was his thumb he was holding up. He was giving me a thumbs-up sign. I pointed to his picture again and gave him a thumbs-up back.

A door opened behind him and a woman came in carrying a mug of tea or something with a straw in it. He had this sort of table across his wheelchair and the woman put the mug down on it and held the straw to Mr Shackleton's mouth. He pulled away and pointed at the window. At me. The woman turned round and started shouting.

'I've told you lads before, now go away before I call the police!'

'No!'

I held *The Wrestler* up for her to see and pointed to the picture on the front. She mouthed, 'Wait there,' and went out of the room. A couple of seconds later the front door opened.

'I'm sorry, love, there's a gang of lads sometimes tease my dad and make faces at him through the window, I thought you were one of 'em.'

I held out the magazine.

'No, I found this and I thought he might want to see it.'

She took hold of it and stared at the cover for a couple of seconds.

'There's more photos inside. Page four, look.'

She looked and smiled at me.

'He is "The White Rose", in't he?'

'He was, before he had his accident.'

What was she talking about? He *is* 'The White Rose'. Just because he's in a wheelchair, it doesn't stop him still being 'The White Rose'. If he *was* 'The White Rose' he still is. She gave the magazine back to me.

'No, it's for him. I want him to have it . . .'

I poured some more gravy over my potatoes.

'Wait till you see it, Doreen, you forget what a handsome man he was.'

They were still going on about the magazine.

'Run upstairs and fetch it, love, while I get the apple crumble.'

I love my mum's apple crumble.

'I haven't got it, I gave it to him.'

'Y'what? Who? What are you talking about?'

'Mr Shackleton – "The White Rose".'

And I told her how I'd gone round to his house while she and my Auntie Doreen had been at church.

'I thought it might cheer him up.'

My Auntie Doreen put her arm round me and gave me a big hug.

'What a lovely thing to do. You see what a thoughtful lad he is, Freda.'

She kissed me. I could smell roast pork.

'I bet he was pleased. What did he say?'

My mum tutted and sort of laughed as she was getting the apple crumble out of the oven.

'Doreen, the poor man can't talk, he hasn't said a word for years.'

She gave me some apple crumble.

'Custard?'

I love custard but only if it hasn't got lumps in it. My mum's is never lumpy, not like school custard.

'Yes, please.'

'I'm sorry, love, but that magazine won't have meant a thing to him, you know. It was a nice thought but you wasted your time.'

What was wrong with them all? It *had* meant something to him. He'd been really pleased. I burned my tongue on the custard.

'Careful, love, it's hot.'

'It's lovely, Mum.'

That's what the woman had said as well, that it wouldn't mean anything to him.

'No, it's for him. I want him to have it.'

The woman looked at the front cover again and shook her head.

'It's very nice of you, dear, but you might as well keep it for yourself. It won't mean a thing to him. He doesn't remember anything about those days.'

But I knew it *did* mean something to him. When I'd shown him the picture through the window he'd given me a thumbs-up sign, hadn't he? It must have meant something to him. I'm sure he remembered.

'I'd like you to give it to him, please.'

She sighed and shrugged her shoulders.

'Well, you might as well come in and give it to him yourself.'

'No, er, I've got to go home—'

She didn't hear me, I don't think she did anyway. She'd gone back down the hall so I followed her into the house and into the front room.

'Dad, there's a young lad come to see you. He's got something for you.'

She talked to him like he was a little baby, really slow and loud, like he was stupid.

'Do you remember when you used to wrestle, Dad? Do you remember? What did they used to call you? The – White – Rose.'

I couldn't understand why she was shouting. He wasn't deaf. He'd heard me when I'd tapped on the window and I'd only tapped quietly.

'The – White – Rose. Do you remember, Dad?'

He just looked at her. His eyes were watery. She turned to me.

'You can give it to him if you like but it'll not mean anything, he doesn't remember. Give us a shout when you've done, I'll be in the kitchen.'

She went. I took *The Wrestler* over to him.

'Mr Shackleton – I found this magazine and I thought you might want it 'cos you're on the front. Look.'

I held it up and showed him the photo of him holding up the champion's belt. I didn't shout like she'd done, I knew he wasn't deaf.

'That's you, in't it, Mr Shackleton? You're "The White Rose", aren't you?'

He looked at it and after a couple of seconds he looked at me and smiled. Then he did it again – the thumbs-up sign. He gave me the thumbs-up sign. See – he did remember.

'Can I have some more apple crumble, Mum?'

She gave me one of her looks.

'Please?'

'That's better. Doreen?'

'No thanks, love, I've had to loosen my skirt as it is. It was all lovely.'

I sat and ate my second helping of apple crumble and custard and thought about Mr Shackleton. I was so glad I hadn't thrown *The Wrestler* away.

THE WHITE ROSE

Part Two

I tap quietly on his front room window. His eyes are closed. He doesn't open them. I tap again, a bit louder. He still doesn't open them. So I tap even louder and he doesn't move, he looks like he's dead. Hell fire, maybe he *is* dead. My stomach churns and I knock on the window, really loud this time. He opens his eyes. I made him jump.

'Hello, Mr Shackleton, sorry if I made you jump. I'm on my way to school. I thought I'd surprise you.'

I've got used to it now, him sometimes being asleep when I go round to see him, but that first time, that Monday morning on my way to school, the morning Tony was off with scarlet fever, it'd really frightened me. I'd really thought he was dead. I hadn't shouted, I'd mouthed at him like my mum does when she sees somebody who can't hear her. She'd done it last Saturday afternoon when we'd passed the hairdresser's and seen Tony's mum under the dryer. She'd mouthed at her through the window.

'How is he? Is he getting any better? Is he still under the doctor?'

Tony'd been off school with scarlet fever all week. Mrs

Wainright had mouthed back. I couldn't tell what she was saying but my mum could.

'What did she say, Mum?'

'He'll be back at school next week, he'll be coming round the usual time.'

Tony's my best friend. He lives two streets away and we always go to school together and he's always on time. But last Monday I'd still been waiting for him at twenty-five to nine when my mum had given me my dinner money.

'You'd better go without him, love, you don't want to make yourself late as well.'

I put my dinner money in my pocket and while I was putting on my coat there was a knock on the front door.

'Talk of the devil, here he is. Come on, love, get your school-bag, it's nearly twenty to nine.'

'It might be Norbert, Mum.'

Norbert Lightowler sometimes tags along as well but he's always late so we never wait for him. It'd turned out to be neither of them, it was Mrs Wainright. She was out of breath.

'I hope I haven't made your lad late, Freda, but our Tony's not well, looks like scarlet fever. I'm going to have to fetch the doctor. Will you tell your teacher when you get to school, love?'

I said I would and I got going. I'd had an idea.

I always try and see Mr Shackleton on my way back from school but when I'm with Tony and Norbert and some of the others I go home first and then I go and see him. I wouldn't want to go round there with any of the other lads, he might think it was that gang that tease him and make faces at him, especially Norbert 'cos that's just what he would do. He's stupid is Norbert.

Mr Shackleton's got used to me coming round on an evening, I think he looks forward to it. But last Monday, when Tony was poorly with scarlet fever and I'd been on my own, I thought I'd go and see him on my way *to* school. You know, surprise him.

I tapped quietly on his front-room window. His eyes were closed. He didn't open them. I tapped again, a bit louder. He still didn't open them. So I tapped even louder and he didn't move, he looked like he was dead. Hell fire, maybe he *was* dead. My stomach churned and I knocked on the window, really loud this time. He opened his eyes. I made him jump.

'Hello, Mr Shackleton, sorry if I made you jump. I'm on my way to school. I thought I'd surprise you.'

I think he could tell what I was saying. Even if he couldn't it didn't matter, he was just pleased to see me. He smiled. His eyes were watering and I waved to him. It's always the same, that's all we do. I wave to him, he smiles, gives me his thumbs-up sign, I give a thumbs-up back, then I go. But it had frightened me thinking he was dead like that.

'What's it like then, scarlet fever?'
    'Bloomin' horrible—'

Another Monday. On our way to school. Tony was better.

'Temperature. Sore throat, you can hardly swallow and my cheeks were all red and your tongue goes red an' all.'

'Everybody's tongue's red.'

I stuck mine out and showed him.

'No, redder than that, really red. Strawberry red, my mum said it were.'

I was glad he was back, Tony's my best friend. But the week he'd been off poorly I'd gone past Mr Shackleton's every morning on my way to school and now I was worried that he'd be looking out for me. I didn't want him to think I'd forgotten about him.

'Oh no – I've left my dinner money on the hall table. You go on, I'll see you there.'

It was the first thing that came into my head. I ran off as if I was going back home, cut through Skinner Lane, ran up Beamsley Lane, turned left by the library, right into St Barnabas Street and then walked the rest of the way to Mr Shackleton's. I'd be all right, I wouldn't be late. Tony and me always give ourselves plenty of time. I just wanted to let him know not to look out for me in the mornings any more.

He wasn't there. There was no one in the front room. It was empty. I'd got so used to seeing him, sitting there at the window, it gave me a bit of a shock.

'What are you up to? No good, I should think, if you're like any of those other tykes that are always hanging round here.'

It was the lady next door. I hadn't seen her come out, she made me jump.

'Go on, get off to school before I call the police.'

'No, I'm lookin' for Mr Shackleton, I always wave to him when I go past, he knows me.'

She looked at me.

'Are you the lad that brought that magazine for him a few weeks back? The one with him on the front?'

I nodded.

'Yeah, *The Wrestler*. He was Yorkshire champion. "The White Rose", they called him.'

She smiled at me.

'That was a right nice thing to do, Brenda told me all about it. Gave her dad a whole new lease of life, she says.'

'Oh . . .'

I wasn't sure what she was talking about, but it sounded all right. She was still smiling anyway.

'You've just missed him, love. He was unwell in the night, Brenda's taken him to the doctor's.'

'Oh.'

'Bit of a temperature, nothing serious.'

I hoped it wasn't scarlet fever.

'Hey, it's nearly quarter to nine, you'd best get off to school, lad.'

'Yeah.'

She picked up the pint of milk that was on the doorstep.

'My friend had scarlet fever, he says it's horrible.'

I don't think she heard me, she'd gone back in the house.

*

113

'Fletcher . . .'

'Here, sir.'

'Garside . . .'

'Sir.'

'Gower . . .'

'Yes, sir.'

While Mr Parry was taking the register most of us were messing about like we always do, he never seems to notice. He never seems that bothered anyway. Sometimes when we have him on an afternoon we can do what we like 'cos he falls asleep. He has this bottle of medicine in his jacket pocket that he has to take and I think that's what makes him sleepy. When I have to take medicine my mum always measures it out on a spoon. Mr Parry drinks his straight from the bottle.

Barraclough was stuffing bits of paper down the back of David Holdsworth's neck, Kevin Knowles and Colin Lambert were playing Cat's Cradle under their desks, Geoff Gower and Norbert were firing paper pellets at each other and Arthur Boocock was giving Keith Hopwood a Chinese burn. Nearly everybody seemed to be mucking around.

'Keep it down while I take the register. Hardcastle . . .'

'Here, sir.'

'Holdsworth . . .'

'Sir.'

I was thinking about Mr Shackleton going to the doctor. I was hoping he was all right. I took some paper out of the middle of my geography exercise book and started drawing a picture of him. I was trying to do the one of him

114

lifting up the belt when he became Yorkshire champion. I thought I'd give it to him on my way home from school but I'm useless at drawing. It looked stupid. It was rubbish. I put a moustache and a beard on him, screwed the paper up into a ball and threw it at Norbert but it missed by a mile so he didn't even notice. That's when I heard my name being called out.

'Yes sir, here, sir, sorry sir.'

'Three times I called your name out, lad, why don't you speak up? I'll tell you why, because you're mucking about like the rest of them. Now keep the noise down while I finish this register. All of you!'

'Yes, sir.'

We all sang it together.

'Yes, sir.'

'That's better. McDougall . . .'

The bell went. Home time at last. I hate Mondays, they're boring. I hate school, every day's boring. I ran as quick as I could to the cloakroom. I wanted to get away before Norbert and Tony and any of the others so I could go straight to Mr Shackleton's on my way home. I needn't have bothered, they were all staying on to play football in the schoolyard. I told them I had to get home. Norbert tried to persuade me to play, they were one short.

'You can stay on for a bit, can't yer?'

I could have done but I wanted to see Mr Shackleton.

'No, my mum's taking me to the chiropodist, I've got an in-growing toenail.'

I couldn't think of anything else. It was the first thing that came into my head, just like in the morning when I'd told Tony I'd left my dinner money at home. I didn't even know what an in-growing toenail was but my Auntie Doreen had been to the chiropodist with hers about two weeks back and it was all I could think of.

'I'd better get going, she'll be waiting for me.'

I couldn't believe it. She'd said he'd had a bit of a temperature, the woman next door. Nothing serious, that's what she'd said. Just a bit unwell in the night. And now he was dead. I couldn't believe it. As soon as I got there I knew. The front-room curtains were closed and I knew. I remembered what my Auntie Doreen had told me the day Mr Bastow had died.

'That's what you do when someone dies, love, you close the curtains.'

'Even when it's light outside?'

'It's custom, love. When someone dies, you draw the curtains. It's a mark of respect.'

I stared at the closed curtains. He was dead. Mr Shackleton. 'The White Rose'. The Yorkshire champion. Dead. And I started crying.

'What's up, love? Has that Boocock lad been hitting you again? I'll swing for him if he has. I will.'

I blew my nose and shook my head.

'No, it's Mr Shackleton, Mum – he's died.'

She didn't say anything for a second, she looked shocked.

'Are you sure? How do you know?'

'I went to wave to him on my way home from school, you know like I do, and his curtains are closed. He wasn't there this mornin' neither, he was poorly, he'd had to go to the doctor's, the woman next door told me. They never close his curtains, Mum, not even when it's getting dark. He likes to look out of the window as long as he can.'

I started crying again and my mum put her arm round me.

'Can we go and pay our respects, Mum, like we did with Mrs Bastow?'

''Course we can.'

'And take some flowers?'

''Course.'

The front-room curtains were still closed. I held the flowers while my mum rang the bell. After a couple of minutes the door opened.

'Hello, Brenda, I've just heard about your dad, I'm very sorry.'

My mum nodded at me to give the flowers. I held them out but she didn't take them.

'Sorry, Freda, heard what?'

My mum looked at me then at her.

'That he's . . . er . . . not well.'

'Well, he's got a bit of a cold and he had a slight temperature this morning. Why, had you heard different?'

My mum looked at me again.

'It's not my fault, Mum.'

I looked up at Brenda or whatever her name was.

'Why did you close the curtains?'

'Y'what?'

'You closed the curtains and my Auntie Doreen told me that's what you do to let people know when someone's died. I thought he'd died!'

If she hadn't laughed I think I would have started crying again. She laughed her head off, she couldn't stop laughing. Neither could my Auntie Doreen when my mum was telling her all about it later on.

'. . . and it turns out, Doreen, they've had some compensation money from the insurance, after all this time, and that's what they've spent it on. A television receiver! That's why the curtains were closed, they were watching it!'

My Auntie Doreen was laughing so much there were tears running down her cheeks.

'Honest, Doreen, I didn't know where to put myself. I could have cheerfully brained him.'

'It wasn't my fault, how was I supposed to know?'

My Auntie Doreen wiped her eyes and took hold of my hand.

'I've got to tell you, Freda, I'd have thought the same. If I'd gone past at four o'clock in the afternoon, and the curtains were pulled to, I'd have assumed there'd been a bereavement. I would.'

She ruffled my hair and gave me a hug and my mum started laughing. So did I.

'Well, it's funny now, Doreen, but I can tell you it wasn't funny half an hour ago.'

I didn't see so much of Mr Shackleton after that. Most days when I went past after school the curtains were closed 'cos he was watching his television receiver. One Saturday afternoon when they were open I saw Brenda giving him a drink. She saw me and mouthed, 'Wait there,' went out of the room and a couple of seconds later the front door opened.

'Do you want to come in and watch the television with my dad? There's a programme just starting, he loves it.'

I went in and Brenda closed the curtains and it was like being at the pictures. I'd never seen television before, not properly. I've looked at all the flickering screens in the television shop in town while I've been waiting for the bus but you can't hear anything, you have to guess what they were saying.

We watched this programme called *Whirligig*, with a funny man with black hair and a puppet called Mr Turnip. It was good. When it finished a voice said, 'BBC Television is now closing down,' and Brenda switched it off and we watched this white spot getting smaller and smaller until it disappeared. I didn't know anybody with a television receiver except Mr Shackleton. It was like a magic box.

'Hey, wouldn't it be good, Mr Shackleton, if you could switch it over to another programme like on the wireless?'

Brenda wheeled him over to the window and opened the curtains. The light made me blink.

'Switch it over! That'll be the day. It's a miracle as it is, looking at someone talking to you in your own front room. The wonders of modern science!'

She went into the kitchen to put the kettle on and I sat with Mr Shackleton for a few minutes. He still had *The Wrestler* magazine on the table across his wheelchair. He pointed at the front cover, gave me the thumbs-up and smiled.

Brenda had said I could go round there and watch the television whenever I liked and I would have done if it hadn't been for my mum. She didn't want me to make a nuisance of myself so I didn't go. I'd wave to Mr Shackleton if the curtains were open when I went past but most times they were drawn to and I stopped going that way, especially after we broke up for Christmas.

'Oh, that's very nice, look at this, Doreen.'

My mum showed her a Christmas card that had been dropped through the letterbox.

'It's from Brenda Shackleton, she's invited us round on Christmas Night to watch *Television's Christmas Party* with Jimmy Jewell and Ben Warriss, isn't that nice of her?'

Jimmy Jewell and Ben Warriss! They're my favourites, I

love Jimmy Jewell and Ben Warriss, I always listen to them on the wireless.

'Am I invited? I love Jimmy Jewell and Ben Warriss.'

''Course you are, look what she wrote on the card.'

My Auntie Doreen passed it over and I read it.

'What *is* a new lease of life?'

I knew it was something good 'cos my Auntie Doreen smiled at me, same as the next-door neighbour had.

'It means when you gave him that wrestling magazine you made him very happy.'

She took the Christmas card back and read it again.

'Hey, Freda, I thought her name was Brenda Jackson?'

'It was, but after her husband left, she went back to Shackleton. He left about a year after the accident . . .'

My mum mouthed the next bit – but I could tell what she was saying:

'. . . told her he couldn't live with a cripple in a wheel-chair.'

It was really funny, *Television's Christmas Party*. It started at half past seven and finished at nine o'clock. Then we had some Christmas cake and we all had something called sweet sherry but I only had a bit. It tasted like medicine. Mr Shackleton liked it, I held his straw for him and Brenda started crying.

'I'll tell you something, Freda, he is good, that lad of yours. Given my dad a new lease of life he has.'

It was a good Christmas.

*

Holidays over. Back at school. Everybody talking about what they'd got for Christmas. Norbert asked me what my main present was.

'I got tons of stuff.'

'So did I, but what was your main present? I got a two-wheeler.'

Yeah, his dad had probably nicked it, he's always in trouble for thieving. So's Norbert.

'It's a Raleigh three-speed. What did *you* get?'

I'd wanted a Meccano set but my mum couldn't afford it. She'd got me a tin of Quality Street, a jumper from the Co-op, some socks, a *Beezer* annual and I'd got a shirt from my Auntie Doreen.

'Come on, you must've got a main present.'

'Meccano set. Big one.'

That shut him up.

'Don't like Meccano.'

And he went off, asking other people what they'd got for Christmas.

About three weeks after we'd gone back it was my turn to be ill. I didn't get scarlet fever like Tony but on the Sunday night I felt awful. I was hot and cold both at the same time and I could hardly swallow, my throat was so sore. Next morning it was worse and my mum had to stay off work to wait for Dr Jowett to come.

He took the thermometer out of my mouth.

'A hundred and three, open wide, say aah . . . again . . . once more . . . Laryngitis.'

He told my mum I had to stay in bed for a few days.

'I don't have to go to that Craig House home again do I, the one you sent me to in Morecambe?'

I didn't want to go there again, Craig House, I hated it.

'No, no. Plenty of fluids, couple of aspirin every four hours and you'll probably be back at school by the end of the week. He's got a mild dose of laryngitis.'

Mild dose! I felt terrible. That first day anyway. On the Tuesday I didn't feel so bad so my mum was able to go back to work and by the Wednesday I was enjoying myself. I was in my mum's bed – I always go in her bed when I'm poorly – I had no temperature and my throat hardly hurt at all. I had my comics, my *Beezer* annual, some grapes and a banana, a bag of pear drops from my Auntie Doreen and a big jug of Robinson's lemon barley on the bedside table.

'Now, I'll be back same time as yesterday to give you your dinner, around half past twelve, all right?'

Yeah, I was all right. Better than school, this. And I had the wireless. I love listening to the wireless when I'm poorly. Specially when I'm feeling better.

'You've got your lemon barley, and your comics and you can listen to the wireless so you won't get bored and Mrs Carpenter from number twenty-three might pop in, just to check on you, all right?'

My mum plumped up my pillows, kissed me on my forehead and filled my beaker with lemon barley.

'You've got no temperature, that's a blessing.'

'My throat's still a bit sore, though.'

I didn't want her sending me back to school too soon.

Mind you, even if I'd gone, I wasn't to know that I'd have been back home by dinnertime. Everybody was sent home early that Wednesday, the whole school.

'Do you want the wireless on?'

'Please.'

She switched it on, kissed me again and went downstairs.

'Bye!'

'Bye, Mum. See you later!'

I heard the front door slam as the wireless warmed up.

'. . . and now at ten to eight it's time for *Lift Up Your Hearts*.' I'd heard that yesterday. Boring. But I couldn't be bothered twiddling with the knob. Anyway, there'd be a story later on. I went through my comics. This looked good. *The Ox-Bow Incident*. A cowboy. Yeah, I'd start with that one, then I'd go on to *Radio Fun* then *Film Fun* and then my favourite, *Captain Marvel*. I always like to leave my favourite till last . . .

I didn't know where I was for a minute. My *Captain Marvel* was open on the eiderdown. I must have fallen asleep. What time was it? I hoped I hadn't missed the story on the wireless. There was just music playing. It wasn't the usual music like they play on *Music While You Work*, it was slow and boring. I wondered how long I'd been asleep? I leaned over to look at my mum's clock. Nearly quarter past eleven. Aw, I had missed the story, it comes on at eleven. I was thirsty. While I was having a drink of my lemon barley the music on the wireless stopped.

'This is London. It is with great sorrow that we make the following announcement.'

It went all quiet for a second.

'It was announced from Sandringham at 10.45 today, February 6th 1952, that the King, who retired to rest last night in his usual health, passed peacefully away in his sleep early this morning . . .'

The King was dead. King George had died. I stopped drinking my lemon barley and put the beaker back on the bedside table.

'. . . The BBC offers profound sympathy to Her Majesty the Queen and the royal family . . .'

I'd only just learned the words to *God Save the King*. We had to sing it every day at school. What were we going to sing now?

'. . . The BBC is now closing down for the rest of the day . . .'

Closing down? No wireless?

'. . . except for the advertised news bulletins and summaries, shipping forecasts and gale warnings . . .'

Shipping forecasts and gale warnings! I wished I hadn't read all my comics.

'. . . Further announcements will be made at 11.45, 12 o'clock and 12.15 p.m.'

Then this dreary music came back on. I didn't know what to do . . . I lay back and stared out of the window . . . It was quite a nice day . . . No it wasn't, the King had died . . . I didn't know what to do . . . Yes I did. 'Course I knew what to do. I got out of bed, went downstairs and

125

pulled the curtains to in the front room. Then I came back upstairs, closed the curtains in my mum's room, got back into bed and lay there listening to the dreary music.

'Why are all the curtains drawn?'

My mum was back, I could hear her coming up the stairs.

'In here as well! What's going on? Why are all the curtains closed?'

She went over to the window and opened one of them.

'The King's died.'

'Y'what?'

'King George. He's died.'

'Oh, don't start all that again!'

And she opened the other curtain.

'It was on the wireless, Mum . . .'

His funeral was on a Friday and we all had the day off school to listen to it on the wireless. We were lucky though, my mum, me and my Auntie Doreen, we watched it on the television. Brenda invited us round with a few other people. She closed the curtains and I sat next to Mr Shackleton.

It was boring but it was better than being at school, I suppose. After we'd been watching for a while, I was holding the straw for Mr Shackleton while he was having a drink, when he pushed the cup away and I thought he'd had enough. He took hold of *The Wrestler* and held it out for me. He probably knew I was bored but it was too dark to read so I whispered to him that it was all right. I thought I was being really quiet but a few people turned round and my mum gave me a dirty look. Mr Shackleton kept pushing the magazine into my hand so I took it. Then he put his mouth towards the straw and I held the cup while he had another drink.

I thought the King's funeral was never going to finish, I could hardly keep my eyes open. At last it was over and Brenda switched it off while my mum and my Auntie Doreen and the others thanked her and said how wonderful it was and things like that. I watched the white spot disappearing.

'Thank you, Brenda, that was a wonderful experience . . .'

'I've never seen anything like it, Brenda, just think, you're in your front room and you're there at the same time . . .'

'I can't get over it, Brenda, wonderful. And that Richard Dimbleby, hasn't he got a beautiful voice? He brings it all to life, doesn't he?'

I couldn't understand what they were all going on about, it wasn't as good as *Whirligig*, I'd been bored as anything. So had Mr Shackleton, I think, 'cos he'd fallen asleep. Brenda opened the curtains.

'Now, who'd like a nice cup of tea? I'll put the kettle on.'

'I'll give you a hand, Brenda.'

'Me too.'

'Let me do it.'

His head was lolling on one side and some spit was

dribbling out of his mouth but it was when I saw that his eyes were open that I realised and ran into the kitchen and whispered to my mum.

My Auntie Doreen took me home while the others stayed to be with Brenda. We were walking up St Barnabas Street and I looked back. Brenda was closing the front-room curtains.

It wasn't till I got home that I realised I was still holding *The Wrestler*.

THE BIRTHDAY PARTY

Reverend Dutton looked at his watch.

'Ah, half past three!'

He looked over at Keith Hopwood and smiled.

'I think this is the moment the birthday boy has been waiting for. Am I right, Mr Hopwood?'

Keith blushed and nodded.

'W-well, it's not my b-b-birthday till M-M-Monday but m-my dad's on n-n-nights next w-week so I'm having my p-party today.'

Reverend Dutton nodded, smiled again and looked round the class.

'Right then, all those of you who are lucky enough to be going to Keith Hopwood's birthday party, please leave now – quietly.'

That's what happens when you're having your party on a school day, you can take in a note from your mum to ask if those who are invited can leave early. The school never says no and it's great if you're one of the ones going. You feel really good leaving early, specially on a Friday after-noon when it's boring scripture with Reverend Dutton. You don't feel so good when you're one of the ones left behind.

'Come on, boys, quick as you can, please, the lesson's not over for the rest of us.'

And today I wasn't feeling so good. I couldn't believe it when Keith had told me I wasn't invited.

'But Keith, I'm one of your best friends, you're always comin' round to my house, why can't I come to your party?'

He just shrugged and said his mum had told him he could ask no more than five.

'Who have you got coming?'

He told me. Boocock and Barraclough? Norbert? Tony? David Holdsworth? I couldn't believe it. Well, I could believe David Holdsworth, he's Keith's best friend, he lives in the same street, just two doors away. And Tony, who's *my* best friend, is always invited to birthday parties, everybody likes him. But why Norbert? And why Boocock and Barraclough? They're always picking on Keith 'cos of his stutter.

'Boocock and Barraclough! Why are you askin' them? You don't even like 'em. They're always pickin' on you.'

He hadn't said anything.

'You're scared of them, aren't you? You just want to keep in with 'em.'

He went a bit red.

'B-B-Boocock s-s-said he'd th-thump me if I didn't invite them. You know w-what he's like.'

I do. It's hard to stand up to Arthur Boocock.

'Well, you could have invited me instead of Norbert.'

'I w-w-would have d-done, honest, but he g-gave me ha-ha-half a crown.'

Where would Norbert have got half a crown from? He'd probably nicked it.

'Where did he get half a crown from?'

Keith just shrugged again.

'Probably n-n-nicked it. Anyway, I've n-n-never b-been to one of *your* b-b-birthday parties.'

'That's 'cos I don't have one. You know I don't, my mum can't afford it.'

My mum's always asking if I'd like a little party at home but I want one like the others have, when you go out somewhere. Tony went to the zoo for his party. Duggie Bashforth had his at the transport museum and we all had tea there, that was one of the best. Geoff Gower's birthday was in the Easter holidays and his mum and dad took a load of us to the fair. Mind you, they've got tons of money, Gower's dad's got a greengrocer's. I never like to ask my mum for something like that though 'cos I know it would cost her too much money.

'If I did have a party I wouldn't invite you!'

Keith just sniffed and shrugged and walked off. It's all right for him, his mum and dad both work, they've got more money coming in.

'Come along, boys, hurry yourselves, I'm sure Mrs Hopwood is waiting for you with lots of jellies and fairy cakes.'

Everybody laughed and Reverend Dutton looked round the class.

'That's what birthday parties used to consist of when I was a lad. Potted-meat sandwiches, fairy cakes and jelly. Then we'd all play Pass the Parcel and Musical Chairs . . .'

He looked a bit sad. I wasn't sure but I think he had tears in his eyes.

'And sometimes we'd play Blind Man's Buff or Pin the Tail on the Donkey. Oh, happy times, we had such fun.'

Boocock snorted and we all started giggling. Keith told him that his party was going to be nothing like that.

'No, w-we're havin' f-f-fish 'n' chips for tea, Reverend D-Dutton, and then w-we're going to the p-p-pictures.'

'Oh, lovely. Well, off you go, have a nice time.'

He picked up his Bible and turned to the class.

'We have to get back to David and Goliath, don't we, boys?'

Everybody groaned.

'Now, where were we? Ah yes, Goliath yelled, "Choose a man from among you to come and fight me. If he can kill me the Philistines will be your servants. If I kill him all of you will become servants of the Philistines . . ."'

Who cared about David and Goliath and the Philistines when you could be having fish and chips and then going to the pictures? I watched them all following Keith out into the corridor. Boocock turned at the door, grinned and gave us all a thumbs-up. Why hadn't Keith invited me? I could understand him being scared of Boocock and Barraclough, but Norbert! Just 'cos he'd given him half a crown? I'm more his friend than Norbert is. Keith's always coming round to my house for tea and stuff. And I'm always sticking up for him, specially when he's being teased 'cos of his stutter. I never tease him like the others do. Like Norbert does. Norbert's always taking him off, pretending to stammer like he does. And then Keith goes and invites him to his birthday party instead of me just 'cos he'd given him half a crown. I wouldn't do that to him. I'd invite him to my birthday party. If I had one.

Reverend Dutton was still going on about David and Goliath.

'Now, boys, Goliath was this thundering giant of a man. He was over nine feet tall and everyone was terrified of him . . .'

Yeah, like Arthur Boocock, we're all terrified of him. Oh, roll on four o'clock . . .

On my way home I had to collect the washing from the launderette. It's in the block of shops near school and I have to take it there every Friday. It's called a service wash, the woman there does it all. I drop it off in the morning on my way to school and then pick it up on my way home. It wasn't so bad when it was just our stuff, I could manage to carry it, but now I have to take my Auntie Doreen's as well. It was my mum's idea after she'd been to that bring and buy sale at St Barnabas Church hall last year.

'Look at that, Doreen, it only cost me a pound at the bring and buy sale. A pound!'

There it was, standing in the middle of the kitchen.

My Auntie Doreen and me looked at it and then at each other and we burst out laughing.

'Well, it may have been cheap, Freda, but I'd say that's a pound wasted. What on earth possessed you to buy a pram?'

'You're not having a baby are you, Mum?'

She gave me one of her looks but I couldn't stop laughing. I wouldn't have been laughing so much if I'd known why she'd bought it.

'This is for you, young man.'

Me? What was she talking about? What would I be doing with a pram?

'And for you, Doreen. There's method in my madness. You'll both thank me.'

I didn't know what she was on about. Neither did my Auntie Doreen.

'Freda, what are you blathering on about? Why would either of us be interested in a pram?'

My mum sat back in her chair and folded her arms. She nodded at me with this big smile on her face.

'Every Friday he struggles to the launderette with our dirty washing, don't you, love?'

Oh no, I knew what was coming.

'And every week, Doreen, you struggle to the launderette with your two bags of washing.'

'Yes, on a Thursday, and it's a real pain I can tell you.'

'Not any more, it won't be, Doreen.'

She pointed to the pram.

'No, Mum, I'm not wheeling a pram to school, it's embarrassing.'

My Auntie Doreen was telling her what a good idea it was.

'I'm not doin' it, Mum. I'm not wheeling the washing in a pram.'

'Freda, that's a wonderful idea. Why didn't we think of something like that before?'

'I'm not doin' it, Mum, they'll all laugh at me . . .'

And they do. Every week. Boocock and Barraclough are the worst of course.

'Have you changed its nappy?'

'Is it a boy or a girl?'

'What's its name?'

Once, when I first started taking the pram, they'd picked up one of the bundles and started throwing it to each other and the dirty washing had ended up all over the pavement. Pants, vests. My mum's undies. All over the place. This lady had to help me collect it all up. It was awful.

Norbert and Keith sometimes tease me as well.

'Aw, l-l-look, Norbert, in't it b-b-bonny . . .'

'When are you havin' another one? You don't want an only baby, y'know, that's what my mam always says . . .'

Even Tony joined in once. He'd found this baby's bottle in the street and put it on my desk when he'd got to school. He did say sorry afterwards.

At the beginning I started leaving home late so that I wouldn't bump into any of them. I'd run like mad, pushing the blooming pram all over the pavement, running round people, and sometimes I'd end up being late for assembly and get into trouble, so now I don't care. If they see me and start saying things I just push the pram and ignore them. And most of the time they don't bother. They've all got used to it. Just shows, if you make out to people that you're not bothered by the things they say, they get bored and leave you alone.

Thank goodness I don't have to take the pram all the way to school, the woman at the launderette lets me leave it with her.

When I got there on my way home from school the washing was all folded up ready for ironing and the woman had put it in the pram.

'There you are, love, I've kept it all separate for you. That's your mum's stuff and that's your auntie's. See you next Friday, love.'

She held the door open for me.

'Ta.'

I wheeled the pram out and started walking up the road. If I've got the money I usually get twopenceworth of chips from Pearson's and eat them on my way home. I stopped, put the brake on the pram and started going through my pockets. Great, I found a couple of halfpennies, all I needed was one more penny. I was feeling in my inside blazer pocket when I saw them in the sit-down bit at the back of the shop. Boocock and Barraclough, Norbert, Tony and David Holdsworth. Keith was sitting between his mum and dad and Mr Hopwood was opening a big bottle of dandelion and burdock. I love dandelion and burdock. They were all laughing and eating lovely fish and chips. I wondered what they were going to see at the pictures. I found a penny in my inside pocket but I didn't buy any chips, I set off for home. I hate Keith Hopwood.

'Mum, you know it's my birthday next Friday?'

She was darning my socks. She looked up at me and smiled.

'Yes, I do know that, I don't think I'm likely to forget your birthday, love.'

She ruffled my hair.

'I can't believe what a big lad you're getting.'

She gave me a hug and kissed me on my forehead.

'I didn't mean that, Mum, what I meant was, can I have a party?'

She looked at me, surprised.

'I asked you if you wanted a party, you said you weren't bothered.'

I wasn't bothered then.

'I've changed my mind.'

I wasn't really that bothered now. I just wanted to have a birthday party so I could tell Keith Hopwood he wasn't invited. And not the kind of party I knew my mum would be thinking about. Mine was going to be different. Thanks to the lady in the fur coat I'd seen on my way home.

I was pushing the pram along Skinner Lane when this big car went over a puddle as it was pulling up. I got water all over my socks and shoes. I was soaked.

'Daddy, Daddy! It was the best birthday party ever, wasn't it, Mummy?'

I looked up and saw these girls coming out of the Rolarena. There were four of them and they were carrying roller skates and one of them was holding a balloon saying 'Happy 7th Birthday'. The girl's dad got out of the car, took the roller skates and opened the back door for them. They all got in, laughing and giggling, saying it was the best party ever. He opened the passenger door for the girl's mum, then went round to the back of the car and put the roller skates in the boot. The lady was wearing a fur coat and she stood on the pavement to take it off before she got in.

'The roller-skating was a huge success, Bernard, and the tea they laid on for the girls was first class, you couldn't fault it.'

As she was getting into the car I saw something drop out of one of the pockets of the coat. It was a piece of white paper. The man closed the boot and walked round the front to get in. Then I realised what it was she'd dropped.

'S'cuse me, mister, this fell out of her coat.'

I held it out for him. He came round, took it and tapped on the passenger-door window. The lady wound it down.

'Darling, look what you dropped in the street – a five-pound note! This young man found it.'

She looked ever so surprised and put her hand on her mouth. The girls in the back were singing happy birthday and laughing. The man had got his wallet out and was putting the five-pound note away.

'It fell out of your coat pocket, missus, when you were getting in the car.'

'Thank you, thank you so much.'

'S'all right.'

I went back to the pram and started wheeling it off.

'Hang on a second.'

It was the man calling me back. He still had his wallet in his hand.

'This is for you. A little reward.'

I went back. *Little!* It was a ten-shilling note. He was giving me a ten-shilling note.

'Thank you. Thank you very much, mister.'

He smiled.

'My pleasure. Buy something for yourself and the baby.'

I didn't like to tell him it wasn't a baby, just my mum and my Auntie Doreen's washing.

'I'll get your Auntie Doreen to do you a cake, she's a better baker than me. I'll do potted-meat sandwiches, they always go down well.'

No. I knew what I wanted to do for my birthday. And I couldn't wait to see Keith Hopwood's face when he found out what he'd be missing.

'No, Mum, I want to have it at the Rolarena.'

'What?'

'You can hire roller skates and they do a first-class tea.'

She looked at me like I was mad.

'The Rolarena?'

'Just a few of us. Me, Tony, Norbert and David Holdsworth, that's all.'

'I'm sorry, love, I can't afford anything like that.'

I couldn't stop myself from smiling.

'I can.'

And I showed her the ten-shilling note. She could hardly believe it when I told her how I'd got it.

Next day we went to the Saturday-morning matinee, me, Norbert, Keith and Tony. Keith was excited 'cos he'd be going up on the stage and getting his ABC Minors birthday card from Uncle Derek.

They were going on about Keith's party, the lovely tea and what a good time they'd had at the pictures and how Mr Hopwood had bought them ice lollies and Butterkist. They'd been to see *Ivanhoe* with Robert Taylor. I love Robert Taylor, he's one of my favourites, I was dying to see it. If Keith had invited me he'd have been coming to my roller-skating party. But not now.

'It's my birthday next week. I'm having a roller-skating party. At the Rolarena. And we'll be havin' our tea there.'

Norbert looked like the lady in the fur coat did when she'd been told she'd dropped the five-pound note.

'Roller-skating party! Oh, I'm comin' to that. I hope. Am I? Can I come?'

''Course you can. There's four of us goin'. You, Tony, me . . .'

I looked at Keith.

'And David Holdsworth . . . Sorry, Keith, my mum says I can ask no more than three.'

I couldn't stop myself from smiling.

When I got home from the Saturday-morning matinee I couldn't believe it. My mum was going on about the ten-shilling note. I couldn't understand what she was talking about.

'I know where you got it from, young man, you were never given it, you took it from my apron pocket, didn't you?'

'What?'

What was she talking about?

'I had a ten-shilling note in my apron pocket and it's gone and you come home with some cock and bull story about being given ten shillings by a man outside the Rolarena. I know where you got it, you took it out of my apron.'

This wasn't fair.

'I didn't, Mum, honest! I was given it.'

I had once taken a threepenny bit out of her apron, ages ago, when I was about nine, and I'd owned up afterwards. But I'd never take ten shillings.

'I didn't take it, Mum, honest.'

She looked at me. I could feel myself going red.

'Why are you going red?'

I didn't know why I was going red. I do that at school when we're asked to own up about something. I go red even when I haven't done it.

'I don't know, I can't help it, but I didn't take your ten shillings, honest.'

'I don't believe you, it's all too convenient this story about a man giving you ten shillings and then suddenly there's a ten-shilling note missing from my apron. You can forget about this roller-skating party now, that is not going to happen.'

I couldn't believe this. It just wasn't fair.

'But, Mum, I've already invited them.'

She started putting on her coat.

'Well, you'll just have to un-invite them, won't you? And don't bother taking your windcheater off, you're coming with me, you can carry my shopping.'

I was holding two heavy carrier bags, waiting for her to come out of Gower's greengrocer's. It's next to Pearson's fish and chip shop and I saw two lads from my school coming out. I turned away, I didn't want them to see that I'd been crying. She just wouldn't believe that I hadn't taken her money, even when I'd said cross my heart and hope to die. I was going to have to tell the others that I wasn't having a roller-skating party now. And wouldn't Keith Hopwood have a good laugh?

My mum came out of the shop and started walking up the road.

'I've just got to pick up a couple of things from the dry-cleaner's and that's it.'

I followed her. I didn't say anything more about the money, there was no point, she was never going to believe me. Then, after we'd gone past the launderette we heard someone calling out to my mum. It was the lady who does the service wash.

'Ee, I'm glad I spotted you, love, I meant to give this to your lad yesterday . . .'

She held out a ten-shilling note.

'I'm not sure if it's yours or your sister's, it was in that pink blouse, in the breast pocket.'

My mum looked at me.

'Oh, love, I don't know what to say, I'm ever so . . .'

I felt sorry for her.

'I was sure I'd put it in my apron pocket, I could have sworn I did. Oh, love, I do apologise.'

She knelt down and put her arms round me.

'We'll go and book it now, we'll go straight to the Rolarena . . .'

Reverend Dutton looked at his watch.

'Ah, half past three!'

He looked over at me and smiled. I'd given him it the day before, the note from my mum asking if the ones going to my roller-skating party could leave half an hour early.

'I think this is the moment the birthday boy has been waiting for, am I right?'

I nodded.

'Yes, sir.'

'Roller-skating party, eh?'

'Yes, sir.'

I looked round the class.

'My goodness, that's very original.'

Keith Hopwood was glowering at me.

'In my day we used to have a little tea party then play games, Blind Man's Buff, Musical Chairs . . .'

We could hardly hear him 'cos of these fire engines outside, racing up the road, clanging their bells.

'Sometimes we'd play Pass the Parcel. That was my favourite, I used to love Pass the Parcel . . .'

More fire engines. Norbert and a few others got up to look out of the window.

'Then there was Pass the Parcel with forfeits. Do any of you still play that? Pass the Parcel with forfeits? It's the same as Pass the Parcel but every layer of paper contains a forfeit, you know, you had to sing a song or eat a teaspoon of mustard, those sort of forfeits. It was huge fun . . .'

Suddenly Geoff Gower shouted out and pointed.

'Sir, look at that!'

Everybody looked. The sky was full of black smoke. We all rushed to the window. There were more fire engines now and bells clanging like anything. We couldn't see any fire though.

'All right, boys, sit down, it's only a fire, back to your desks, please.'

Norbert was standing on the pipes to get a better look.

'Looks like a big one, sir, look at the sky.'

Reverend Dutton made him get down.

'It'll probably be one of the mills. The fire brigade are on their way, that's the main thing. Right, all those going to the roller-skating party can leave. Quick as you can, please.'

Now it was my turn. I went to the front of the class and Tony, Norbert and David followed me. I turned at the door and took one last look at Keith. He looked fed-up. Serve him right!

My mum had said she'd meet us by the school gates around twenty to four. She'd asked if she could leave work early and I was hoping she wouldn't be late. She'd booked the party for four o'clock and we were going to meet my Auntie Doreen there. We were standing by the gates, waiting for her, watching more fire engines racing up the road. There were police cars as well. The sky was getting blacker and blacker. It was quite exciting. This workman was walking past and Norbert asked if he knew what was going on.

'Oh, it's massive, lad, huge fire, must be nine or ten fire engines.'

We asked him if it was one of the mills.

'No, thank goodness. It's the Rolarena – went up like a tinder box. All wood, y'see. It's gone. Burned to the ground. There's nowt left.'

That's when I heard my mum. She was running up the road.

'I'm here, love! Sorry I'm late. There's been a big fire. No buses. I had to walk. Anyway, we'll be all right, we'll get there by four.'

We went to Pearson's for fish and chips and then to the pictures. *Prisoner of Zenda*. It was all right. But not as good as roller-skating.

THE TRICK

'Where are *you* then, love? I can't find you.'

We were looking at the school photo. We had it spread out on the kitchen table, it was about three feet long. I was holding one end and my mum was holding the other.

'Over there somewhere, Mum, at your end.'

'I can't find you.'

'I think I was next to Keith Hopwood.'

'That's a big help, where's he?'

'I can't remember, it was ages ago when they took it.'

I leaned across to look where I was on the photo. I took my hand off my end and it rolled back up into a scroll.

We'd got them that afternoon. Mrs Garside, the school secretary, had brought them in during scripture and Reverend Dutton had handed them out at the end of the lesson.

'Now, boys, you'll be pleased to know that in this box, kindly delivered to us by Mrs Garside, is at long last the eagerly awaited school photograph.'

'About time, we paid for 'em ages ago!'

'Thank you, Boocock, we know we've been waiting a

while for these, and stop leaning back in your chair like that, take your feet off the desk.'

Boocock stared at Reverend Dutton and slowly did as he was told. As soon as he was sitting up straight Barraclough did the same thing, leaned back in his chair on two legs and put his feet up on his desk. Reverend Dutton looked at him, you could tell he didn't know what to do. He turned round, picked up the box of photos, then looked back at him. Barraclough still had his feet on the desk. So did Boocock.

'Stay behind afterwards, the two of you, we're going to have a little talk.'

They both laughed. They wouldn't stay behind, they just do what they like in scripture, we all do. You can get away with anything in Reverend Dutton's class.

He started coming round handing out the photos. They were all rolled up and held together with a rubber band.

'Now, don't open these here, boys, wait till you get home. They're very long, you'll get into a terrible mess.'

'Course everybody ignored him and started looking for themselves and laughing.

'Holdsworth, you've got your eyes closed . . .'

'Look at Gower, he's doin' a V-sign . . .'

'You'll get done for that, Gower . . .'

'Look at Jackie Parry – he's fast asleep . . .'

'Who's that idiot? You can't tell who it is, he moved . . .'

The photographer from London had told us we had to keep dead still while the photograph was being taken.

*

'This is not like a normal camera, it's a special camera to take panoramic photographs. It'll move from one side to the other, so you have to keep dead still . . .'

We were all in rows right across the playground. There were about six rows of older lads at the back standing on different-size tables – it must have taken the caretaker ages to set it all up. Then there was a row of chairs for all the staff and sixth-formers.

'We use this special camera at schools all round the country. It'll start taking the picture on *my left* and move all the way across to *my right* and you must keep *dead still* . . .'

First and second years were right at the front. Second years had been told to kneel and we were sitting on our bums. I was between Keith Hopwood and Duggie Bashforth.

'You mustn't move a muscle and that includes the teachers . . .'

Everybody laughed, well, those who'd been listening. That's when Ogden, the headmaster, got up.

'Quiet!'

We shut up quick.

'This gentleman has come all the way from London to take our school photograph. It is important you listen to instructions. Carry on.'

He went back to his chair that was right in the middle and the photographer from London carried on.

'Thank you, Mr Ogden. As your headmaster has just said, it's very important to listen to my instructions. The camera will move from left to right. When I start the exposure it will take about forty-five seconds. Do you think you can keep still for forty-five seconds?'

'It's you, Cawthra, you moved, you couldn't even keep still for forty-five seconds!'

'It isn't me, I'm over there next to Emmott!'

'Oh. Who is it then? You can't tell . . .'

Reverend Dutton was still going round handing out the photos. I didn't unroll mine, I wanted to wait till I got home.

'One for you, Lightowler, the last one.'

Norbert hadn't been at school that day. You'd had to wear a school tie and a school blazer to be in the photo. He didn't have either.

'Not mine, sir, I'm not gettin' one. I'm not on it. I was off sick.'

'Oh, that's a shame, Lightowler.'

'Yes, sir, it is, sir.'

Reverend Dutton held up the last photograph.

'Have I missed anybody out?'

'No, sir . . .'

'Well, there's one left over, it must belong to someone.'

It went quiet. We all looked at each other. It was McDougall who put his hand up.

'It'll be Manningham's, sir . . .'

Reverend Dutton didn't know what to say for a minute. He went a bit red.

'Oh yes . . . yes, of course . . . Er, yes . . . I'll, er . . . yes . . .'

That was the last day Manningham had come to school, the day of the photo.

'Who's that, love, holding two fingers up to the camera? That's not a nice thing to do on a school photograph, is it?'

I was looking for Manningham. I couldn't find him.

'Geoff Gower. He said he was copying Mr Churchill.'

My mum looked at me.

'I don't think so. Anyway, it's *Sir* Winston Churchill now.'

'Oh . . .'

Where was Manningham? I was finding it hard to remember what he looked like.

'Ooh, my Lord, who's this? Look at his hair!'

'Who?'

'One of the teachers. I've never seen hair like it.'

She was looking at Reverend Dutton.

'Scripture teacher. He wears a wig.'

I carried on looking. Where was he? My mum was still going on about Reverend Dutton's wig.

'Poor man, someone should tell him, it looks ridiculous.'

There he is! There was Manningham, right at the end of the row – smiling.

'Take a card, any card . . .'

Norbert was watching out for Melrose while our class stood round in a group, watching Manningham doing another of his amazing tricks.

151

'Any card you like . . .'

Boocock pushed everybody out of the way.

'I'll choose it!'

He's always the chooser is Arthur Boocock, we never get a look-in.

Manningham turned away from us towards the black-board, covering his eyes.

'Don't show it to me, Mr Boocock, but remember the card.'

He calls everybody mister when he's doing his tricks. When he'd first come into our class I didn't know what to make of him. I'd thought he was a bit barmy, off his head. I didn't like him. He was a show-off.

'Memorise that card, Mr Boocock, make sure everybody sees it.'

He's not a show-off, though, he's just different. Different from anybody else in our school.

Boocock held up the card. It was the eight of Diamonds.

'Does everybody know what the card is?'

We all shouted 'Yes' except for Norbert.

'I don't, I'm over here looking out for Melrose, what is it?'

Manningham still had his back to us. 'Don't shout it out, Mr Boocock! Would you please show Mr Lightowler the card?'

Boocock held it up.

'Has Mr Lightowler seen the card?'

'Yes!'

We all said it together again.

'Then please replace the card into the pack that is sitting on the table. Anywhere in the pack, please.'

Boocock picked up the cards and pushed the eight of Diamonds into the middle.

'Now get on with it, Manningham, before Melrose comes.'

Manningham turned round, opened his eyes and looked at Boocock.

'You can't hurry magic, Mr Boocock.'

He took the cards and started to shuffle them.

I wish I could be like Peter Manningham. He's not scared of Boocock and Barraclough like the rest of us. He's not scared of the teachers. He's not even scared of Melrose. You could tell that from the very first day he'd come into our class.

'Leedale?'

'Here, sir.'

'Lightowler?'

'Sir.'

'Manningham?'

We'd all turned round to have a look at the lad who had been kept down. He should have been in the year above.

'Oh dear, Manningham. Relegated, were we?'

'I'm afraid so, sir, one of those things.'

And he'd just smiled at Melrose.

'Well, go on at this rate, lad, and you'll be in your twenties before you leave school.'

Melrose had looked round the class with his lip curling like it does and we'd all laughed. Not 'cos we'd thought it was funny – 'cos we knew Melrose expected us to. Manningham had just smiled again.

'You're dead right, sir. But don't you agree, there's always two sides to everything, sir? Advantages and disadvantages. Hopefully when I do leave, Mr Melrose, I'll be better educated, won't I?'

That's how he talked to teachers. If it'd been me or Norbert or any of the others, we'd have got clouted or kept in after school, but not Peter Manningham. He seemed to get away with anything. With everything.

'Not if you get expelled, you won't, and that's what'll happen if you don't sort yourself out, lad!'

Manningham had just smiled that smile of his.

'I'm now going to lay these cards on the table, face down. I will turn each card over until I come to the card that Mr Boocock chose.'

We all stood round the table, watching as he started picking them up. King of Clubs, six of Hearts, nine of Spades. How would he know that it was the eight of Diamonds Boocock had chosen? It was impossible. We all leaned in closer. Jack of Diamonds, five of Spades, two of Clubs . . .

'*What* may I ask is going on here?'

Stupid Norbert! Instead of looking out for Melrose like he was supposed to, he'd come over from the door and was watching with the rest of us. Everybody ran to their desks. Everybody except Manningham, he just carried on turning over the cards. Norbert looked at Boocock. He knew what was going to happen to him at break.

'Manningham! Collect those up and get to your desk!'

He didn't even look up. He just kept turning the cards over, showing each one to the class before he put it into the other pile. Eight of Spades, queen of Diamonds, four of Diamonds. He wasn't even hurrying.

'Just give me a couple of seconds, sir. We are coming to the climax of an amazing bit of magic.'

That's what I mean. You don't talk to teachers like that, especially not Melrose. You wouldn't even talk to Reverend Dutton like that. But Manningham did and he got away with it.

King of Diamonds, ace of Hearts, five of Clubs. He stopped turning over the cards and looked up at Melrose for the first time.

'Just a little bit of your time, sir, that's all I need. I think you'll be very impressed with this.'

He didn't even wait for Melrose to reply. He just smiled his smile and carried on picking up the cards, showing them to us and putting them aside.

Seven of Spades, nine of Clubs, king of Hearts. Still no eight of Diamonds. Melrose didn't say anything, he just stood there watching like the rest of us. That's when it dawned on me. That's how he got away with it. It was the way he always smiled at people after he'd said something. It was like magic. It was the same that day when he hadn't done his homework for Bleasdale.

*

'Frankly, young man, I'm not surprised that you've had to stay down a year, this is quite intolerable.'

Manningham had nodded.

'You're dead right, sir, but if you remember the weather was lovely last night, really mild and it was either doing my Latin homework or taking my granny out for a walk – she's in a wheelchair, sir, and she doesn't get out much and I thought, no, I'll take her for walk and honestly, sir, it did her the world of good . . .'

And there it was, the smile. And he wasn't putting it on, you could tell, it's just the way he is. Bleasdale wasn't sure what to say.

'Yes, well . . . er, that's very commendable, Manningham, it is important to look after your grand-mother, but listen, lad, I do want you to do that work for me, perhaps you could do it tonight.'

Manningham hadn't said anything for a couple of seconds, it was like he was thinking about it.

'I'll try, sir. I'll do my best.'

I'll try? I'll do my best? If any of us had said that we'd have been crucified, but not Peter Manningham. People just like him.

'Good lad, you can only do your best.'

Good lad? You can only do your best? God, I wish I could be like Peter Manningham . . .

He was still picking up the cards. Four of Hearts, ace of Clubs, ten of Clubs . . . there weren't many left.

'Well, gentlemen, we are coming to the end of the pack and I haven't yet found Mr Boocock's card.'

Boocock snorted.

'Well, I put it in there. Everybody saw me.'

Manningham carried on turning the cards over, showing us each one before he put it into the other pile. Seven of Hearts, three of Diamonds, eight of Clubs.

'Then, Mr Boocock, your card must be here.'

King of Spades, three of Clubs, five of Diamonds. Ten of Hearts, nine of Hearts, seven of Clubs . . . No eight of Diamonds.

'Gentlemen – there is only one card left. This, then, must be Mr Boocock's card!'

What a fantastic trick! How did he know which card Boocock had picked? And how did he make it the last card? How could he make sure it was at the bottom of the pile after he'd shuffled them? It was magic. He put his hand on it.

'So, gentlemen, this is the card chosen by Mr Boocock!'

He picked it up slowly and showed it to us . . . jack of Clubs! Jack of Clubs? It was the wrong card, he'd mucked it up.

'That wasn't my card, mine wor the eight of Diamonds.'

Everybody agreed with Boocock. Manningham was frowning, he couldn't understand it. I felt sorry for him.

'But that was the only card left. It can't have been.'

Boocock sneered.

'You're useless, Manningham!'

Barraclough, Hopwood, Norbert and some of the

others started jeering. They soon shut up when they saw Melrose looking at them.

Manningham was going through the pack of cards. Melrose put his hand on his shoulder.

'Come on, lad, let's get this lot cleared away, we've wasted enough time.'

Manningham was still looking at all the playing cards.

'You see, there is no eight of Diamonds here, but I believe Mr Boocock when he says that is the card he put back into the pack.'

Melrose started pushing Manningham over to his desk.

'Yes, well, I wouldn't believe everything "Mr" Boocock tells you, now come on, lad, let's get on with the lesson.'

Manningham held up his hands. 'The thing is, gentlemen, if Mr Boocock's card *was* the eight of Diamonds, where has it gone?'

Everybody groaned. The vein under Melrose's eye started to throb. If Manningham wasn't careful he was going to get a clout. I felt so sorry for him.

'Look, Manningham, you just need to practise a bit more. Now go and sit down before I lose my temper.'

'Mr Melrose! Would you please do me the honour of looking in the right-hand pocket of your jacket?'

Everybody stopped talking. Melrose looked at Manningham. We all looked at Melrose. No, it was impossible. The eight of Diamonds couldn't be in his pocket, we all saw Boocock put it in the middle of the pack. Oh no, Manningham was making a right fool of himself.

'Mr Melrose, would you please place your hand in the right pocket of your jacket and tell me what you find there?'

It was dead quiet. I looked around. Everybody was staring at Melrose. How could it be in his pocket? There was no way . . .

'I hope you're not wasting my time, lad.'

He was. He must be. There was no way . . . Melrose felt in his pocket and the vein under his eye started to throb again and he looked at Manningham. He pulled his hand out of his pocket and, yes, he was holding a playing card. Melrose looked at it, then showed it to us. The eight of Diamonds. It was magic.

For a second you could have heard a pin drop, then everybody started cheering and Melrose was slapping Manningham on the back.

And there it was again, that smile . . .

'Well, I still can't find you, love.'

I was looking at Manningham in the photo, wishing he was still in our class. I missed him.

'Look at this teacher, *he* looks like he's fast asleep.'

I didn't have to look. I knew who that was. History teacher. Jackie Parry. He wouldn't have even been in the photo if it hadn't been for Peter Manningham . . .

We were all watching him, trying not to laugh. His head kept dropping forward on to his chest, then he'd suddenly sit up straight and look at us like he didn't know where he was for a minute, then start falling asleep again. Once

Jackie Parry was asleep we could do what we liked, till then we had to make out we were reading whatever he'd told us to.

'Time for my medicine, boys. You know it tends to make me a bit sleepy, so while I close my eyes for a few minutes I'd like you to read the chapter on Martin Luther and the Reformation. Page seventy-one. Answer as many of the set questions as you can, boys.'

I used to think it really was medicine he had to take. I used to feel sorry for him, I hate taking medicine.

It's always the same when we have him in the afternoon, specially on a Friday when it's the first lesson after our dinner-break. When we have history on a Tuesday morning we really have to work, he never falls asleep then.

His head started dropping again and some spit was dribbling down his chin. Norbert couldn't help laughing and Boocock thumped him on the back of his neck and showed him his fist. I'm glad I don't sit in front of Boocock.

It was Norbert who'd told me what it was Jackie Parry was really drinking.

'Y'what?'

'It's whisky, like what my dad drinks.'

'What's that?'

'It's like beer, only stronger. He's an alkie is Jackie Parry.'

I hadn't known what he was talking about.

'What's an alkie?'

'Someone who likes drinkin'. My dad's an alkie.'

He'd said it like it was something good. Norbert had

told me all about his dad, how he hits him when he's been drinking. I hadn't known that's what they were called. Alkies.

'My mum says it's like they're poorly, that alkies can't help it, they have to drink.'

'They don't have to hit you. Jackie Parry doesn't hit anybody.'

Norbert had looked at me.

'No, he just falls asleep. There's different sorts of alkies . . .'

Jackie Parry was snoring now. Boocock went up to him and waved his hand in front of his face . . . then he tapped him on the shoulder . . . then he gave him a little push . . . he was fast asleep. Great, we could do what we liked.

'Hey, Ma-Ma-Manningham, d-do another of your tr-tr-tricks.'

Manningham smiled.

'Not tricks, Mr Hopwood, it's magic.'

We all started chanting.

'Manningham! Manningham! Manningham!'

We chanted quietly. Not 'cos we were worried about Parry waking up – we weren't bothered about that, but we didn't want to get him into trouble. It'd turned out that the headmaster knew Jackie Parry was an alkie and that Parry could lose his job 'cos of it. Me and Norbert had overheard the head talking to Melrose in the corridor outside the cloakroom one night after school. I'd had to go back for my windcheater. I'd got all the way home when I realised I'd left it on my peg. Norbert had come with me 'cos he'd had nothing better to do.

'He's an excellent teacher, I agree. First rate. But let's face it, Jack Parry's got a drink problem, he's an alcoholic.'

We heard Melrose telling the headmaster that it had only got worse since his wife had died.

'And he's fine in the mornings, Headmaster. Perhaps we could re-schedule his lessons.'

'I can't organise the school timetable around Jack Parry's drink problem, Brian. If he doesn't do something about it, he's going to have to go!'

Norbert and me had to stop ourselves from laughing, we didn't know Melrose's name was Brian.

'Manningham! Manningham! Manningham!'

I sat at the kitchen table looking at his smiling face in the school photo, thinking about that afternoon when he'd saved Jackie Parry from getting the sack.

'Manningham! Manningham! Manningham!'

Manningham stood up, went to the front of the class-room and held his hands out. We all went quiet. Without saying a word he took a piece of string from his pocket and held it up to show us.

'A simple piece of string, gentlemen.'

He tied a knot in it and wrapped it round the back of

his hands like he was going to do Cat's Cradle. That's what Boocock thought he *was* going to do.

'Cat's Cradle? Oh, brilliant trick, this, I don't think!'

Manningham took no notice. He wound the string round again so it was double.

'And now, gentlemen, I would like a volunteer.'

We all shouted at once.

'Me! Me! Me!'

'Mr Lightowler – would you please step forward?'

Norbert went up to the front with a big grin on his face. Manningham was holding the string with both hands.

'Mr Lightowler, would you take those scissors on Mr Parry's table and cut the string in two between my hands.'

'S'all right. I'll use my penknife.'

He's a fool, Norbert, we're not supposed to bring knives to school. He cut the string and Manningham told him to sit down again.

'So you see, gentlemen, I am now holding separate pieces of string.'

He held them up in his left hand and the loose ends dangled down.

'I am now going to tie these lengths of string together using only – my teeth!'

His teeth! How could he tie two pieces of string together with his teeth? It was impossible!

Using both hands he put the ends of the string in his mouth. We all sat watching. After about a minute he slowly started pulling one end of the string back out of his mouth. He kept pulling and when he'd pulled it right out, there it was – the string all in one piece, like when he'd started. It was magic, just like the eight of Diamonds.

Nobody could believe what he'd just done for a minute. Then we all clapped and shouted and those that could, whistled.

I think it was Holdsworth who must've seen him first 'cos he sits right by the door. All I know is I was still clapping and cheering when I heard someone shout, 'Ogden!' It went dead quiet. Nobody knew where to look. All you could hear was Jackie Parry snoring . . .

'And as you see, gentlemen, Mr Parry is now hypnotised!'

We all sat there gawping. Manningham was still at the front of the classroom, and he was pointing towards Jackie Parry. Melrose had come in as well now and was standing next to the headmaster. I could see Mrs Garside out in the corridor behind them.

'I will now bring Mr Parry out of his deep sleep. He will not remember anything.'

He went over to Jackie Parry's chair and started to wake him up gently.

'Three, two, one. Wake up, Mr Parry. Three – two – one! Wake up, Mr Parry!'

Jackie Parry opened his eyes and he looked like he didn't know where he was for a minute. We all just sat there. Manningham turned round to the headmaster.

'I shouldn't say this, Mr Ogden, magicians aren't supposed to give away their secrets, but just in case you're worried, I didn't really hypnotise Mr Parry. It's a trick it, Mr Parry?'

And he smiled . . .

'Fancy falling asleep like that on a school photograph. You wouldn't credit it, would you?'

'It's Mr Parry, Mum. History teacher. He was ill. He's left now.'

I don't think he got the sack. He went off one Friday dinner time a few weeks ago and never came back. Melrose told us he'd decided to give up teaching. Bit like Manningham, he went home after the school photo and we never saw him again.

'Ah, I've found you, love, there you are! Oh, you do look handsome. Very smart. We'll have to get this framed.'

I looked all right, nothing special. Me and Keith had these stupid grins on our faces.

'Mum – that's Peter Manningham, there.'

I pointed him out.

'What a grand-looking lad.'

I could feel a tear running down my cheek. I couldn't help it. I missed him. My mum put her arm round me.

'I miss him, Mum. Why did he have to die?'

She squeezed me tight.

'I know, love, it's horrible. He had a hole in the heart, love. He was born with it. There's nothing anybody could have done. It could have happened at any time.'

'It's not like Mr Bastow or Mr Shackleton, Mum, they

r was only young, he was only a year older

another squeeze.

but I thought it. Why did it have to be
Why couldn't it be Boocock or Barraclough? Why
couldn't they have had a bloomin' hole in the heart?

'He could do magic, Mum. Real magic.'

She smiled and gave me her hanky.

'I'll get your tea ready.'

I blew my nose and looked at the photo again. Poor
Jackie Parry . . . Stupid Gower doing a V-sign, I bet he'll
get the cane for that . . . Why was Illingworth wearing his
school cap? Nobody else was wearing a cap . . . I looked at
me and Keith again . . . That's when I saw it. His last bit of
magic. I couldn't believe what I was seeing.

I unrolled the photo and looked back at Peter. There he
was at the beginning of the row, smiling. I looked at the
end of the row – and there he was again, kneeling with the
second years. Smiling. Grinning. He was on the photo
twice! He must have run round the back.

'Mum! Do you want to see some real magic?'

I wish I could be like Peter Manningham.

Rave reviews for *The Fib* and *The Swap*

'The stories have so much strength and depth
that you want more' *The Times*

'The stories are excellent . . . Layton performs the neat trick
of writing from his own experience in a way that speaks
directly to the children of today' *TES*

'Funny and moving . . . a rare gift' *Guardian*

'An excellent book' *Daily Telegraph*

'Well worth waiting for . . . This is a book about
childhood as well as for children, and equally
successful on both counts' *Independent*

'Gently humorous . . . struggles with complexities of early
adolescence . . . The dialogue rings so true that readers will
hear their laughter echoing' *School Library Journal* (USA)

'Angst, cringing embarrassment and, above all, humour
ensure that this still has children in stitches today' *TES*

'Excellent . . . funny . . . a good mix of fun,
action and adventure' Calum MacDonald (11),
Daily Telegraph – YT section

'Funny, ironic, sad and nostalgic;
but better than those things, it has the smell of truth'

Also by George Layton

The Fib and Other Stories
The Swap and Other Stories